Slave

to the

Past

Book 11 in the Charlotte Diamond Mysteries Series

www.cyberworldpublishing.com

This book is copyright © 2019
Olivia Stowe asserts her right to be known as the author of this work.
First published by Cyberworld Publishing in 2019
Cover design by Cyberworld Publishing © 2019
Cover photo: Copyright Olivia Stowe
E-book ISBN: 978-0-9953873-7-9
Paperback ISBN: 978-0-9953961-2-8

~

Slave

to the

Past

Book 11 in the Charlotte Diamond Mysteries Series

by

Olivia Stowe

Table of Contents

Character List

In 1773

Isata: captive slave girl, transported to South Carolina Colony from Sierra Leone, 1773

Otta: Isata's lover in Africa, 1773

Cuffee: Slave driver on the Oak Ridge Plantation, Daufuskie Island, 1773; son of Hannay

Hannay: Slave woman on the Oak Ridge Plantation, Daufuskie Island, 1773; mother of Cuffee

In 2019

Charlotte Diamond: Retired senior FBI agent; married to Brenda Boynton/Brandon

Brenda Boynton/Brandon: semiretired major movie actress; married to Charlotte Diamond

Chance Diamond: Charlotte's brother; Williamsburg doctor

Marilyn Diamond: Chance's wife; minister

DeeDee Yance: Movie starlet who had had designs on Brenda's son, Tony Trice; newly married to Daufuskie Island-based rock star, Trent Nichols

Tony Trice: Movie star; Brenda's belatedly acknowledged son, born of a teenage affair shortly before Brenda went to

Hollywood and took it by storm; husband (although not declared publicly) of pro tennis player, Michelle Minor

Craig Little: One-time best friend of Charlotte's younger brother, and more significantly, of Charlotte's first husband, Sydney Morrison

Michelle Minor: Pro tennis player and Tony Trice's wife.

Aaron Woolridge: A producer of several of Brenda Brandon's movies, retired to Charleston, South Carolina

Cheryl Chandler: Not so friendly actress colleague of Brenda's. Aaron Woolridge's new wife

Hannay Mongin: Executive director of the rebuilding Charleston International Film Festival

David Burch: Hunky Talbot County, Maryland, deputy sheriff, based in Hopewell, Maryland, where Charlotte and Brenda live and have established a retirement home for movie folk; newly wed to Charlotte's former FBI assistant, Margaret Fancel

Margaret Fancel, Charlotte's former assistant at the Annapolis, Maryland, FBI office, newly wed to Hopewell, Maryland, deputy sheriff, David Burch

Trent Nichols: Rock star living on Daufuskie Island. Recently married to movie starlet DeeDee Yance

Douglas Dolan: Former Brenda flame, architect of their movie folks' retirement home, Curtain Call; lives to sail and lives on his yacht

Steve McCall: Novelist living on Daufuskie Island

Evan Worthington: Head agent of the Annapolis, Maryland, FBI office; Charlotte's former boss and would-be significant other

Otta Stephens: reporter for the *Savannah Morning News*

Maria Silva: Brazilian prostitute

Benjamin Schmidt (Butch): A foreign mercenary soldier and pilot in Afghanistan; now a security guard

Shirley Elgin: FBI agent in charge in Savannah, Georgia

Chapter One: Welcome to the Low Country

Daufuskie Island
South Carolina Colony
3 May 1773

Isata, shackled at her wrists and hobbled at her ankles, was pulled, not too gently but also not too roughly, out onto the deck of the small wooden vessel. She still, as before, wasn't being treated as roughly as the other slaves on the boat were. The pier she found herself on seemed to lead nowhere but to towering oak trees on a heavily foliaged embankment. As nervous and fearful as the beautiful young woman, who had been in Sierra Leone, in Africa, just a few weeks earlier, was, she couldn't help but be taken with the change in her surroundings. Cypresses, sycamores, magnolias and, especially, palmettos and flowering oleanders crowded on the land before her, a shock after the weeks being held in a dark cabin while at sea across the Middle Passage in the English slaver ship. The foliage was new and exotic to her. The land wasn't. It was the same marshy land she knew at home. She had no way of knowing that she had landed on Daufuskie Island, one of the South Carolina Colony barrier islands, at its most showy time or that those towering oaks provided the timbers for the construction of fighting vessels such as the ship that would be the USS *Constitution*.

Farther along the embankment to either side she would have seen what she was familiar with—rice paddy fields—if night wasn't falling. Rice was the staple crop in her own land, and her people were proficient in growing and harvesting it. This was the main reason why the English slavers preyed upon her people and snatched many of them to transport to South

Carolina and Georgia as slaves—to work in the rice paddies and indigo fields there as they did in their own land.

Although closely supervised in her native Sierra Leone on Africa's rice-growing Windward Coast as a perfectly formed eligible young woman, there she was free and unfettered. Here, somewhere in the New World that had been whispered about in her village with fear, she most decidedly was not.

Isata was lucky to be alive. Many who had been transported in the slaver vessel from Africa to the colonial America coast had not survived the ocean journey, which had first landed in the nearby port of Beaufort off the Port Royal Sound. Isata had been lodged in a dark, windowless cabin, along with three other young women. She was fortunate, though, that the cabin was above deck, while most of the Africans taken as slaves—men and women alike—had been virtually stacked in the holds. Her conditions, although dire, were nothing like those of the slaves who were locked up below for the two-week sail. She and the other beautiful young women were segregated and held in less squalid conditions, as they had been separated off to serve the sailors during the crossing and later to be sold for something very different than rice planting and harvesting. They were taken periodically from their shared cabin to an adjoining one for the men's sport.

This is what separated Isata from the other category of slaves to be sold at auction at the Chalmers Street slave block in Charleston, to the north, or the River Street slave market just to the south in Savannah, Georgia. Most of the slaves were brought to this area of the coast to be sold to work in the rice, cotton, and indigo fields. Particularly beautiful and well-formed young women like Isata, however, were brought here to be sold into the brothels of Charleston, Beaufort, Bluffton, and Savannah. Isata was destined for Savannah, and thus had been taken off the English ocean slaving vessel at Beaufort and transferred with other slaves destined for one of the ten rice plantations on Daufuskie Island or the other islands or lowlands bordering on the Calibogue Sound. The owner of the island plantation to which she'd been brought also supplied brothel slaves to the surrounding towns, including the city of Savannah just to the south of the island.

The small vessel had landed at the pier leading off from Pappys Landing Road, off Mungen Creek, close to the southeast tip of the Daufuskie Island. The landing area was called Bloody Point because this was the shoreline where, between 1715 and 1717, the Spanish had encouraged the indigenous native Yemasee people to stage three last-gasp unsuccessful attempts to dislodge the English settlers from the island. This now was the Oak Ridge Plantation, one of ten on the island, where the Mongin family not only grew rice but engaged in the slave trade, supplying slaves, through their contacts with the English slavers headquartered on Bance Island in the Sierra Leone River, to the regional and Savannah markets.

The plantation's black suboverseer, himself a slave called a driver, Cuffee, had come on board the small vessel first and performed an initial assessment of the captives. After he looked them over, he took Isata gently by the arm and led her off the boat and onto the pier. He was a tall, strapping, muscular young buck in his late twenties.

Seeing another face such as hers and hearing him speak to her in something approximating her own Sierra Leone Krio dialect, Isata was somewhat calmed. Still, his size and muscularity were intimidating to her, and, although he let her move at her own pace, he did not free her of the shackles on her wrists or the hobbles on her ankles. It was only as he led her away, up Pappys Landing Road, toward the main complex of the plantation buildings, that other plantation workers, supervised by white overseers started bringing those destined to be field slaves up from the boat's holds and leading them to pens closer to the island's shore than where Isata was being led.

The boat had arrived at the Oak Ridge Plantation pier at dusk, and, although Cuffee didn't lead Isata too far, in the direction of the water to the east, into the woods from Pappys Landing Road, it was pitch dark by the time they arrived at a group of high-fenced pens. The stockade walls of the pens were made of eight-foot-high rough-wood planks. There were maybe four pens with walls abutting each other. Cuffee led Isata into one of these, which was about twelve or fourteen feet to the side, and gestured over toward a lean-to, open-fronted shed at the opposite end from the gate. A thin mattress, stuffed with what Isata would learn was Spanish moss and covered with a cotton cloth, lay on the beaten-earth floor of the shed. Next to the bed were two buckets, one filled with water and with a dipper in it. The other to be used as a necessary. There was a hunk of bread and two small apples on a slab of wood on the mattress. Cuffee unshackled her wrists and left her there, alone, leaving by the gate and securing it behind him.

She was of mixed emotions to see him gone. He was dark, like her, and unlike the sailors who had brought her here and used her during the sailing and he spoke her language, Krio, enough for her to feel she hadn't left her world altogether. But he was such a towering, muscular man that he intimidated her. Also, if he was roaming free here, he wasn't like her.

It was the first time in weeks that she had been alone, though, and had space enough to move around, even if still hobbled. She sank onto the mattress, dipped water to drink, and then dug hungrily into the bread and the apples, not having eaten anything even that fresh for weeks. She paused to touch the ivory bracelet on her wrist, amazed that she still had it after these weeks of captivity, abuse, and torment. The bracelet was composed of a series of oblong ivory disks, held together with leather string knotted into holes in the edges of the disks. Each disk had a design carved into it. Isata knew that Otta, a talented artist, had done the carving herself. One disk had Isata's name and another one Otta's. Other disks bore images of the bush elephant, a monkey, a hippopotamus, and a couple of birds.

As she ate, she thought back to when she had received this bracelet, no more than a month and a half ago. The images in her mind went to Otta, another young woman of her village, and how that day, the last she'd seen Otta, had begun so gloriously and ended so tragically. The two young women had been drawn to each other, and in ways they had to keep secret. They met on occasion in private. The morning Otta had given Isata that bracelet they had lain together and been discovered by Mingo, Otta's brother, who had been courting Isata, unsuccessfully, himself. Mingo went into a rage, beating both young women, taking Isata by force, and then tying her wrists and ankles, slinging her over his shoulder, and taking her down to the river, to his dugout boat. He paddled down the river, to

14

the mouth of the waterway, and then to the island, Bance Island, which the English slave traders occupied. He sold Isata there, getting a good price because of her beauty. She was transported within a couple of weeks across the Middle Passage and eventually reached here, this small stockaded pen located she knew not where in the world. Her world had been lost.

She knew what she was meant to be now, though. Mingo had shown her that, as had a couple of the English slave traders on Bance Island, and the sailors on the ship, and now, she assumed, even the slave driver Cuffee would take his pleasure. She was cursed with extraordinary beauty and sensuality. There must have been some reason she was separated from the others, just as she had been on the ship bearing her across the Middle Passage. She'd seen the look in the ebony suboverseer's eyes when he'd first spied her on the boat at the island pier and then again here in the stockade before he had left. She knew he would be back.

And she was right. It was very soon thereafter that Cuffee was back, naked, slipping into the pen and taking a stance that told Isata she had no way of escaping, nowhere to go. He advanced on her until he was standing close to her. She stood her ground, looking into his eyes, not wanting to look anywhere else. He reached out and unknotted the strip of cloth binding her skirt to her waist and let the material drop to the ground. The deep groan that came up from his depths when he saw her naked told Isata all she needed to know concerning where this was going.

With a sigh, Isata went back to the mat and lay down on her back. She had done this many times in recent weeks, and it was best gotten over quickly. There really was no use struggling against it. Cuffee stood over her for a moment, drinking in the beauty of her sleek ebony body. He leaned down and released her of her hobbles, and then he came down on top of her and covered her. It helped her to take him by remembering the touch of Otta.

He was still on top of her, moving, when a gunshot was heard in the not-so-far distance. Cuffee leaped up and ran to the stockade gate. The gate was ajar and Isata saw that he had left his breeches and rifle just outside the gate. He struggled into his breeches, grabbed up his rifle, and sprinted off toward where the gunshot had come from. In turn, Isata jumped up from the pallet, took up her skirt, and slipped out of the gate and into the forest. She headed in the other direction from the one Cuffee had taken. She had no idea where she was going other than away. She struggled through the foliage for some time, likely going mostly in circles, panting and gasping, before her adrenaline wound down, her strength gave out, and she sank to the forest floor. When she had calmed down, she wrapped her skirt around her more firmly and looked around in all directions, trying to decide what to do now, where to go, how to remain free for as long as possible.

When her heart had stopped pounding in her ears, she found that she could hear the surf. The need to get to the sea became an imperative for her, and she began stumbling in that direction through the undergrowth. She saw the weak, wavering light before she came into the small clearing, where she saw a hut built of tabby, a composition strange to her but one she would learn of, the type of cement made of lime from burned oyster shells mixed with sand, water, ash and crushed oyster shells that predominated on the island. The cottage was perched just inside the foliage line of a short beach leading down to the sea. The light was from a lantern inside the hut as seen through an open door on an otherwise blank wall. She must have been heard thrashing around in the forest, because, as she approached, the frame of a large, well-padded black woman filled the doorway to the building.

"Help me," Isata croaked in Krio.

To Isata's relief, the woman appeared to understand her and answered in a variation of the same dialect. "What is the matter, child? Come inside. You look half dead."

Less than a half hour later, Cuffee appeared at the woman's door.

"What was that gunshot I heard," she asked him, standing squarely in the door frame, which she filled.

"We brought fresh slaves in today, Hannay," he answered. "One of the new field slaves broke away. He was shot. Another one, a young female, has escaped too, though. Have you seen any sign of a young female around here?"

Hannay stood solidly in the doorway, looking her son in the eye, taking her time answering him.

Chapter Two: Too Many Coincidences

The conversation at the joined brunch tables of the large group of diners at Bistro 17 was revolving around Charlotte Diamond's sister-in-law giving some history of the island when Charlotte saw the two from her past—but from entirely different rooms of her past—sitting together across the restaurant from her at another table. Eight friends, also from different rooms of Charlotte's life, were among the other ten who were sitting at her table at the restaurant on the yacht basin underneath the two condos Charlotte and loved ones had taken at Shelter Cove on South Carolina's Hilton Head Island.

Everyone in attendance at the larger table was there at Charlotte Diamond and Brenda Boynton/Brandon's behest and to celebrate their presence in Hilton Head. Charlotte Diamond, a statuesque, handsome woman in her late sixties, who is most politely described as formidable, and Brenda Boynton/Brandon—"Boynton" her given surname and "Brandon" her stage name—a legendary platinum-blonde-haired beauty and actress in movies and the theater for four decades, now in her early sixties, had met incongruously when both were in retreat for different reasons. Charlotte, a highly regarded and successful senior FBI agent in the Annapolis, Maryland, office was coming off a failed marriage, with her criminal husband on the lam, and Brenda was escaping from Hollywood, where she had been outed as a lesbian and accused of murdering her partner. Both arrived ten years previous in the then-sleepy, historical Choptank River village of Hopewell, Maryland,

Charlotte quickly having been elected to, stuck with, according to one's view, the position of the town's mayor and Brenda returning to her ancestral manse in a town where her family had reigned since it was founded.

The two very different women had quickly melded as Charlotte brought Brenda out from underneath her cloud of criminal suspicion in Hollywood and the two learned that being together was better for them both than anything else they could do in life. When Brenda won the Maryland lottery six years earlier, she and Charlotte had combined their resources to establish Curtain Call, a heavily underwritten retirement community for indigent elderly former workers in the movie industry, in Hopewell, to also help revitalize the town. Later that year Charlotte and Brenda had married and since then had lived and vacationed together in an adventuresome life that somehow, often accidently, continued to include sleuthing and movie making.

For Charlotte's Williamsburg doctor brother, Chance Diamond, and his minister wife, Marilyn, also at the table, this was a needed vacation from busy professional lives, but one that had been interrupted by adversity. For Charlotte's wife, legendary movie star Brenda Brandon, this was a vacation mixed with movie festival appearances in nearby Charleston and Savannah as favors for a friend. On the surface, this was a vacation for retired FBI senior agent, Charlotte, but, as often was the case, it wasn't what it appeared to be on the surface for her.

The quartet often vacationed together. Just as often when they vacationed together, they also got wrapped up in intrigue together. At least three of them were hoping to avoid that this time. What they also wished to avoid was what Charlotte, Brenda, and Marilyn continually teased Chance about that vacations with him also included dead bodies and hurricanes. Indeed, it had been a hurricane going through South Carolina four years before that had canceled their previous planned visit to Hilton Head and sent them instead to yet another mystery atop Virginia's Blue Ridge Mountains that Charlotte and Brenda had to solve. Chance, in turn, accused Charlotte as being the source of that family curse.

As Marilyn had been talking about her family's past on Hilton Head, Charlotte had been appreciating that, of the ten people at the cobbled-together table, only she and the newlywed couple she and Brenda had brought on this trip with them weren't here in some sort of convoluted slave to the past dilemma—at least that was what she thought at that moment.

Up until she spied the diners at another table in the restaurant who made her some sort of connection point of relationships here, Charlotte had been feeling like a spectator off to the side at the table. But she liked it that way. She willingly went through life these days in the shadow of her wife, the glamorous movie star, Brenda Brandon, and she'd come to Hilton Head seemingly, at least, to drift around in the background of what brought her significant others here. She often fulfilled the role of background support for Brenda taking the public spotlight. Charlotte didn't mind being in the background. She preferred that role. Many had been the criminal who regretted seeing her in that role as well, because they often didn't know she was tracking them down until she had.

But here Charlotte was, looking across the restaurant and seeing an incongruous gathering at another table. One of the men looked familiar in an entertainment celebrity way, not to mention that she'd recently seen his photo in a file—and God knows they'd been seeing a lot of those types here on Hilton Head this spring—but she knew the woman he was with. DeeDee Yance was sure to complicate matters for others at Charlotte's table, especially the movie star Tony Trace, who was having his own troubles with women in his life already. But the real surprise, the one that might just complicate her own life, was the shock of seeing the third person at that table, a face from her own past.

Craig Little had been the best friend of Charlotte's younger brother, and more significantly, of Charlotte's first husband, Sydney Morrison. The two of them had lived to be in increasingly more serious trouble—trouble that Charlotte had always had to get them out of until it got serious enough to be involving the police. What shocked Charlotte now, in seeing Craig in such an incongruous setting, was that it had often been

Charlotte's experience that when she saw Craig, Sydney was rarely far away.

The last time Charlotte had seen Sydney, he was on the lam from both the feds and the mafia. As a retired FBI agency herself—who could have turned Sydney in at one time but didn't—Sydney was the last person Charlotte ever wanted to see again, in Hilton Head or anywhere else. Suddenly, she was just one more person at the table whose past was catching up with them.

Charlotte's brunch companions already had enough drama in their lives not to be bringing in others. Although the Diamond quartet, as Charlotte, Brenda, and Charlotte's older brother and wife called themselves, had planned to vacation here in Hilton Head, that's not what they were telling people brought them here this May. Charlotte was here because Brenda was here to lend publicity clout to a couple of entertainment endeavors. She was doing a couple of "my movies" nights and was to play in a charity golf tournament leading off the annual RBC Heritage Golf Tournament played at the PGA Sea Pines Plantation Golf Course on the southern tip of the island.

The movie nights were at the invitation of Aaron Woolridge, a former producer of some of Brenda's movies who had retired to nearby Charleston but still had a hand in movies, and the golf outing was because the professional tennis pro, Michelle Minor, was also playing in the tournament. Michelle was the significant other of Brenda's love child, Tony Trace, born of a teenage affair shortly before Brenda went to Hollywood and took it by storm. She was here mainly because Tony and Michelle were having difficulty in their marriage, which, for professional reasons, hadn't been publicly declared yet, and Brenda, who liked Michelle a lot, wanted to bolster that relationship. If only they went public with it, she thought, the marriage would solidify. Until it did, it had a danger, as all Hollywood marriages did, of being incomplete and dissolving.

Looking over to where DeeDee Yance sat, Charlotte was now worried that Brenda's efforts would become more difficult. DeeDee, who was also a movie actress, had been Tony's flame before he had started his relationship with Michelle. The movie press hadn't completely given up on the Yance-Trice romance.

What in the hell was DeeDee doing here, Charlotte wondered. Did she know that Tony was here and that he and Michelle were having a rough patch? Was DeeDee here to make matters worse? That was totally in keeping with the young woman's personality.

Also at Charlotte and Brenda's table was the movie producer, Aaron Woolridge, who had wanted Brenda to do a couple of movie nights in Charleston and Savannah. Having gotten her here, though, he only now had revealed that he had a part for her in a period movie starting production in Charleston, tentatively titled "Gentlemen Pirates," which would play on the 1790s period in Charleston, South Carolina, when pirate kings lived there as prominent citizens without revealing their source of wealth. This version of the movie plot would bring the story to a boil when a Charleston pirate king coveted the beautiful wife of the new governor sent over by the English king for the South Carolina colony.

As Brenda was here to aid her son's cause with Michelle, feeling guilty at not having acknowledged him as her son for years, and because she was trying to retire from films, Aaron's mission was a source of tension. They were very old friends, though, so Brenda was torn. It didn't help that Aaron had brought his new wife, the actress Cheryl Chandler. Brenda and she went way back as well, but it had been Cheryl who strongly counseled Brenda not to acknowledge that Tony was her son. Charlotte only wished that Tony, also sitting at this table, had never been told that.

That left four people at Charlotte and Brenda's brunch table, whose lives also intertwined with those of Charlotte and Brenda. Another reason Charlotte was here at this particular time was that her older brother, Chance Diamond, and his wife, Marilyn, were here, looking at houses. They were considering moving to Hilton Head, after years of being established in the Williamsburg, Virginia, community, where Chance was a doctor and Marilyn a minister. Marilyn's family had been one of the ones that had established Hilton Head as a resort destination, though, and for some reason she had a "return home" notion locked in her brain. Both Charlotte and Brenda were afraid that the source of that was the possibility Marilyn had breast cancer, a

22

possibility that she only now was beginning to fight. They were afraid that Marilyn thought she wanted to die where her family roots were. Neither Charlotte nor Brenda thought that was a good idea—letting herself be possessed by such a morbid idea. The two were well established in the professional communities in Williamsburg and that's where their support base was. The best Charlotte could do was to be here while the couple weighed their options and give them such support as she could.

Sitting between Brenda and Michelle, and paying close attention to both, was a young, gorgeous and confident black woman, Hannay Mongin, who was the new executive director for the Charleston International Film Festival, which had closed down three years earlier and which Hannay, a native of the area who had attended SCAD, the Savannah College of Art and Design, had been hired to try to revive. Through Aaron Woolridge she had landed Brenda to speak at an abbreviated festival this month that featured Brenda's movies. She had come to Hilton Head to coordinate Brenda's appearance with her.

The last couple sitting at Charlotte and Brenda's Bistro 17 brunch table was composed of the newlyweds who were here as a present from Brenda and Charlotte. David Burch was a deputy sheriff—Brenda and Charlotte's favorite law enforcement officer—in Hopewell on the Choptank, the Maryland riverside town where Brenda's ancestors had lived and Charlotte had retired to from an Annapolis office FBI Agent position and where the two women had first met. Through Charlotte, he had met Charlotte's former assistant in the FBI, Margaret Fancel, and after several years as friends, the two had married. They were honeymooning here in Hilton Head at the behest of Brenda and Charlotte. With luck, Brenda had thought, they wouldn't get embroiled with the overlapping dramas of the rest of them. She was taking no bets, though, and Charlotte knew otherwise. It seemed that, despite her retirement from fighting crime, crime seemed to find Charlotte wherever she went.

Margaret had asked Marilyn whether pirates had ever operated out of Hilton Head.

"Not that I know of," Marilyn answered, "although there was piracy all up and down this coast as far north as Delaware.

23

Charleston was a center of taking in the booty—we'd call it laundering these days. The city grew rich off the resale of pirated goods. But I guess that's what your new movie is about, isn't it, Mr. Woolridge?"

The producer nodded and looked at Brenda. "What Brenda's new movie is about too, I hope."

"Now, Aaron," Brenda said, "you know I'm trying to retire."

"But you'll be able to wear Southern Belle costumes," Cheryl Chandler said, with a tinkling laugh that seemed to have been stolen from Brenda, who had been famous for it. "You never could turn down the opportunity to wear period costumes."

"The slave trade ran up and down the coast here too," Marilyn continued.

"Hilton Head dealt in slave running?" David Burch asked.

"Not so much Hilton Head as the island to the south, Daufuskie Island," she answered. "It was closer to the mainland and hidden behind Hilton Head. It was more remote—it still is. Just the Gullah, mixed ancestry country folk, and celebrities in coastal compounds live there now. There's no road bridge to it. Everything still has to come in by boat."

"Daufuskie Island? The island between here, Hilton Head, and the river Savannah is on? That's where your family is from, isn't it, Hannay?" Aaron Woolridge asked, turning to the young black woman he knew in Charleston.

"Yes, from back in the seventeen hundreds," Hannay answered. "From plantation time then. My ancestors were slaves on one of the first plantations on Daufuskie—Oak Ridge Plantation. I have a cottage there that has been in my family since they were slaves on the island."

"And was there slave running on the island back then, do you know?" Margaret asked.

Hannay gave her a long stare, which visibly embarrassed Margaret a bit, before answering, "Certainly not that I heard about."

"That's a beautiful bracelet you're wearing," Brenda remarked, obviously trying to thaw some sort of frozen nerve that had been touched. The bracelet, which Hannay was showing prominently on the wrist of an arm raised to her shoulder, was indeed eye arresting. "I've been looking at that since we sat down for brunch," Brenda continued. "Is it ivory? And are those inscriptions of animals and some exotic language."

"Yes, this bracelet has been handed down to me through the generations," Hannay answered, clearly pleased that Brenda had noticed it. "It has had to be restrung several times, but the ivory disks are original, and we've always used leather, as with the original, for the string. Family legend is that it came over from Africa with the first of my ancestors who was brought here. The writing is in Krio, a language in Sierra Leone. I'm told they probably are names."

"It's beautiful," Brenda said.

"Thank you," Hannay answered, clearly having forgotten now whatever Margaret had said to irritate her.

Marilyn was giving her dissertation on her own family's history on Hilton Head, and the group's attention refocused there. Charlotte leaned over and whispered to Brenda, "Don't look now, but that's DeeDee Yance over at that table with those two men. I should recognize one of the men." Charlotte decided not to mention that she certainly recognized the other one, her former husband's sidekick, Craig Little. Brenda didn't need to know about him, unless it was necessary. Charlotte had periodically seen the FBI file on him and it wasn't good news.

"I know. I saw her. I knew she'd be here. That's one reason I decided I had to be here too. She's married to that guy now. That's the rock-style singer, Trent Nichols. He lives on Daufuskie Island—the place Marilyn is talking about. He's giving a concert in conjunction with the golf tournaments and playing in it as well, I believe. As soon as I read that DeeDee had married him and figured she'd be here the same time Tony and Michelle were, I knew I had to be here too to help run interference. I don't know who the guy is they're talking to."

OK, it was unavoidable. Charlotte wasn't going to keep secrets from her wife. "I do," she said. "That's Craig Little. He always ran with Sydney."

"Sydney? Your husband Sydney?"

"Yes. They were inseparable when they were younger. If Sydney was in on a scheme you could bet Craig was too. And vice versa. Craig flies airplanes. I assumed he flew in and swooped Sydney away when the feds and mafia were closing in on Sydney on that casino scam he tried to run."

"You don't think Sydney could be here too, do you?" Brenda asked.

"Let's not even think about that," Charlotte said, her eyes scanning the outdoor seating area of the restaurant lest her former husband had shown up. "But, god, they're all coming back to roost. There's one for you over there, Brenda."

"Who? Where?" she said and then she gave a deep whistle. "Could that be Douglas Dolan over at that other table?"

"That would be my guess," Charlotte said. It was more than a guess; Charlotte knew he'd be here. She just didn't know he'd be in the same restaurant they were in this evening and she hadn't known how to let Brenda discover his presence on Hilton Head. Douglas Dolan was the architect who designed Curtain Call, the rest home for movie folk that Brenda and Charlotte had financed and opened in their town of Hopewell. Dolan, who also sailed yachts and was a handsome devil, had pursued Brenda for a time, but it had been Charlotte who had won the star.

"I wonder what he's doing down here," Brenda said.

"Well, we know he loves yachting," Charlotte answered, "and we're sitting a few yards away from the Shelter Cove yacht basin. Maybe he's just passing through."

"Perhaps," Brenda said, "a more interesting question is why he has his head so close together with Steve McCall?"

"Steve who? The other man at that table?"

"You don't know who Steve McCall is? That's right, you were an FBI agent but you didn't read crime thrillers. Steve is a novelist. He lives on Daufuskie Island too. He's playing in the celebrity golf tournament. But OK, having all these people in this same restaurant who we know and are connected with in some way is just a coincidence, isn't it? I mean, this isn't working up to another working vacation for us, is it?"

In fact, Charlotte did know who Steve McCall was—she just had never seen him before.

"I wouldn't be too sure about that," she said, deciding that any attempt to keep Brenda in the dark on an aspect of their being in Hilton Head was now a lost cause. "Look who's standing over at the entrance to the restaurant."

Brenda swung her face over in that direction. "Oh my god, it's Evan Worthington. The cast is now complete." She immediately wondered how long he'd been standing there and how much of what they were discussing he'd heard. The answer was long enough, and quite a bit.

Evan Worthington was the head agent of the Annapolis, Maryland, FBI office. He had taken that position in the hopes of taking up with his old flame, Charlotte. But he had come back into Charlotte's life to woo her too late. She had already been won by Brenda. The best that he'd been able to manage, after much effort, was to get Charlotte to agree to continue to consult for the Annapolis FBI office. Since she'd agreed to that, the consulting had stepped on every vacation she and Brenda had tried to take.

"Maybe he's not here for me," Charlotte said in a weak voice that didn't convince even her.

"What was I saying about too many coincidences?" Brenda muttered morosely as the handsome FBI agent walked toward their table. Brenda started to rise to greet him, but Charlotte pulled her back in place and hissed, "Pay him no attention." She was looking beyond Brenda to the rest of the table to see if anyone else noticed. Margaret Fancel, who worked for Worthington, obviously did see him, but she glanced at Charlotte and then called over to Tony Trice to ask him a question. Tony hadn't been paying attention to much of anything because Michelle, sitting beside him, was deep in conversation with Hannay Mongin, sitting beside her, and Tony seemed a little ticked.

Although he'd been making a beeline for Charlotte's table, Evan passed them right by, having come from the inside dining room, and continued out onto the walk bordering the Shelter Cove yacht basin. He had said nothing in passing or indicated that he had seen Charlotte and Brenda at all. Brenda gave Charlotte a quizzical look. "I'll explain later," Charlotte whispered. "Act like you didn't see him." Acting was one of many things Brenda did superbly, so that was not a problem.

In walking by the table, Evan brushed up against a young woman at yet another table in the restaurant who represented yet another thread in this tapestry, one that neither Charlotte nor anyone else in the restaurant that evening was aware of. Before Evan jogged her arm and apologized to her before continuing, the young woman, Otta Stephens, reporter for the *Savannah Morning News*, had been studying the ivory bracelet on Hannay Mongin's wrist, comparing it to a rough sketch of a bracelet she held in her hand.

Ever the perfect lady, as their own dinner group was breaking up, Brenda went over to the table where DeeDee Yance and her new husband were sitting. She congratulated DeeDee on her recent marriage. An actress in her own right who had been in movies with Brenda, DeeDee didn't indicate that she had been working on marrying Brenda's son, Tony, right up until her engagement to the rock star, Trent Nichols, had been announced and that she, no doubt, knew Brenda was aware that DeeDee had been after Tony and that Brenda had not approved.

"And it's good to meet you at last, Trent," Brenda said, leaning over to shake the man's hand. "I was looking forward to that from the moment I found out we were both playing in the golf tournament. I haven't seen the foursome matchups yet, but it would be wonderful if we were in the same one."

"Yes, it would," he answered. "I've been excited to see you as well. You're a legend in the movies." He was speaking that to her breasts as she leaned over to shake his hand and was giving a little grin of approval. He wasn't a young man—more than a few had said he was too old for DeeDee, but he was still what those in the rock fan clubs considered sexy, if rugged looking with a tinge of the effect of heavy drug and sex use. But it was obvious from the way he was ogling Brenda that he didn't consider her too old for him. "Where are you staying while on Hilton Head?" he asked.

"Why, right here, upstairs from here," Brenda said. "You live on Daufuskie Island, I hear—only accessible by boat."

"True, and it seems primitive, but we have quite a colony of celebrities with vacation homes over there and all the

28

amenities one would want. Two golf courses even. You should come across and practice golf with DeeDee and me before the tournament."

"That would be lovely," Brenda said, "but I don't have a boat."

"I do. You could come over for a couple of days. There are plenty of beds." He said that more than a little suggestively and DeeDee gave a little chuckle.

"Yes, do come over, and bring Charlotte with you," DeeDee said, perhaps with a tinge of maliciousness.

"Charlotte?" Trent asked.

"Charlotte is Brenda's wife. She's a retired FBI agent," DeeDee said, quite pleased with herself.

"Oh. Well, yes, of course you both must come for a few days," Trent said. The repeated invitation wasn't quite as enthusiastically given as the original one had been, though.

DeeDee laughed, with a smile that went up to a sparkle in her eyes.

Chapter Three: In the Night

Leaving the dinner at Shelter Cover, Hannay Mongin climbed into her Mini Cooper convertible, drove out to the William Hilton Parkway, and then headed south to Arrow, turning west to an out-of-the way bar, Pegg's, on Dunnagans Alley. Entering the club, she went directly to the bar, perched on a stool, and ordered a Margarita from a chocolaty brown woman bartender who greeted Hannay as a regular customer. A woman saxophonist, also ebony, was playing under a dim spotlight beside a small platform on the other side of the room. There were a few other patrons in the place, marked off as couples—again, all women of color.

Hannay had only been at the bar long enough to receive her drink when another young woman, Otta Stephens, came in and perched on a stool next to Hannay.

"Mind if I sit here?" she asked Hannay.

"Not at all. Did you follow me here? I saw you at Bistro 17 just now."

"Yes, I'll admit that. I followed you here. If that disturbs you, I can turn around and leave."

"It doesn't disturb me. It flatters me—depending on why you followed me, of course."

"I found you quite striking. I think I'd like to get to know you. Can I buy you a drink?"

"I have a drink," Hannay said, raising her Margarita glass to show it off.

"Perhaps the next one, then?"

"Perhaps, if I stay around. Did you follow me here just because I'm quite striking? You're not nervous being in a bar like this?"

"Because everyone is of color and is a woman?" Otta asked, with a smile.

"Yes. But I have no trouble seeing that you are a woman."

Was that a pass being met with a pass back?

"Not at all. I pass, but my ancestors were slaves in Savannah. Just ones attractive to white men for a couple of generations. And I prefer the company of women to that of men."

"Ah, rather direct," Hannay said, saluting Otta with her Margarita. The bartender had materialized and Otta ordered one of the same—and another one for Hannay, who nodded and smiled.

"You were pretty direct with your questions," Otta said when the bartender walked off. "Perhaps you find me attractive as well."

"Perhaps I do. Does that frighten you?"

"Not in the least," Otta answered.

"So, is that the only reason you've followed me here?"

"No. That's one reason, but there is another—another form of mutual need."

"And what would that be?" Hannay asked.

"You are trying to revive the film festival in Charleston, aren't you? You are the executive director for that, I believe. I recognized you from press reports, and I couldn't help hear you discuss it at the restaurant. You were dining with the movie star, Brenda Brandon, because she's doing a program for you, weren't you?"

"Maybe I was dining with her because she is a beautiful and desirable woman, even at her age—perhaps *because* of her age," Hannay said, giving a deep-throated laugh.

"Yes, she's all of that," Otta said. "But I believe you are here on business—discussing her film program in Charleston."

"You seem to have researched me and the Charleston film festival."

"I have. I'm a reporter with the *Savannah Morning News*. I'm doing a report on Brenda Brandon's appearance at a fundraiser for the Savannah Film Festival later in the fall. I thought I would combine it with your efforts to revive the festival in Charleston. My reporting would provide your project with publicity."

"You're researching this because you're interested in a rival festival in a nearby city?" Hannay asked, her face showing amusement.

"That and because I'm interested in you and writing this up will put me next to you."

"How close next to me do you want to get?" Hannay asked, with a throaty laugh.

"Very close next to you," Otta said. "You were asking me if I knew what sort of bar this was. I do. Can I buy you that second drink?"

"Of course. Afterward would you like to come back to my hotel? My room at the Omni Oceanside has a very nicely stocked minibar." Hannay asked.

"And a nice bed?"

"A gloriously comfortable bed, yes."

* * * *

"Marilyn certainly seems to be deep into her family history on Hilton Head," Brenda said in sotto voce. Marilyn and Chance, Charlotte's sister-in-law and brother, were in the other bedroom in the Harbourside condo two stories up from Bistro 17, where they'd had dinner, and Brenda didn't want Marilyn to hear the worry in her voice.

"Unusually so," Charlotte said. She was sitting on the bed, watching Brenda, in a robe, at the desk doing her elaborate nightly hair-brushing routine. Her luxuriant platinum-blonde hair was one of the traits that once had the movie star being called the most beautiful woman in the world. "Perhaps unhealthily so. I hadn't realized she was taking this cancer possibility so hard."

Charlotte rose and came in behind Brenda, reaching around to touch her breast and leaning down to kiss her on the neck. Brenda leaned her head to one side to receive the kiss. Almost as if connecting the action with the concern, she said, "Well, her mother died of breast cancer ten years ago."

"Chance is a doctor and Marilyn has always been careful with her health. Even if it is cancer, they will have caught it early. Marilyn's mother didn't find out quickly and then resisted doing what had to be done. When we invited them to come on this vacation, I didn't think she might have a hidden reason to accept—that this was where she came from, where her mother still lived when she herself was diagnosed, and that her mother's doctor was here. I had no idea that Marilyn would want to consult with her mother's doctor, and that she would want to come back here. She's been almost morose about ending up back where her family came from."

"I didn't think about it either," Brenda said, "but when I did think about it, I realized we didn't really invite them to come with us. Chance just said they wanted to and we vacation together so often that I didn't think twice about it. I did know that Marilyn had established a good relationship with her mother's doctor."

"I think it's ominous that they even are planning on looking at houses down here," Charlotte said.

"Well, we can discuss that with them at breakfast. What you have me really curious about just now is that act with Evan at dinner—him being here, and him wanting you to see him but just walking by us in the restaurant without acknowledging us. You have secrets of your own about this vacation, don't you? When I was thinking about how Marilyn and Chance got invited, it made me think about you. You're the one who suggested we come down here now, aren't you? My golf tournament and film festival appearances were set up later because we'd already be down here. You have something going with Evan, don't you?"

Charlotte moved her hands to Brenda's shoulders. She leaned down and kissed the other woman on the neck again. "You know Evan and I didn't get to first base—when you and I were at third."

Brenda laughed. "Don't try to change the subject. I know that you once were on third with Evan. I'm not being jealous. We both have a past. But there was the cryptic message on your phone when we came back to the condo. I could hear it. It was Evan's voice. Just a time and a place. You're doing something for Evan and the FBI down here, aren't you?"

"Yes, I can't tell you much about it now, but, yes, I'll be doing some nosing around down here for Evan. But you'll be so busy with the golf tournament and film nights that you won't even notice it. It's just as well that I'll have another activity to occupy me while you're off Hollywooding."

"I guess it's just as well that I didn't agree to us spending a few days on Daufuskie Island then."

"You've—we've—been invited for a stay on Daufuskie?" Charlotte was quick to ask.

"Yes, DeeDee Yance and her new husband, Trent Nichols, have a place on the island. Trent and I are in the golf tournament together. And, yes, you were invited too. I think Trent was making sort of a pass at me when he invited me and DeeDee obviously thought so as well. She was quick to point out that there was a you in my life and to invite us both. But I—"

"I think that's a great idea. I think you should accept—that we should accept."

Brenda turned in her chair and gave Charlotte a sharp look. "You think that's a great idea? That's not like you. You're a hermit when you can get away with it. And you don't like DeeDee Yance any better than I do. I'd do it to keep her occupied and away from Tony while he's going through this difficulty with Michelle. But you've always said you can't stand to be in the same room with her. On Daufuskie you'd be on an island with no road out with her until a boat could come pick us up."

"I've heard about Daufuskie. I think it would be fun to spend a few days there."

"Fun? A virtually isolated barrier island? Fun for a city girl like you?" She paused and then gave a little tinkling laugh. "This is about whatever you and Evan are cooking up, isn't it?"

"Maybe," Charlotte answered, but she grinned and quickly changed tact. "But no more talk now. I'm tired. Let's get into bed."

"Are you really tired?" Brenda asked, giving her tinkling laugh that decades of movie goers had come to love and identify with her.

"Not a bit, no. Let's get into the bed," was Charlotte's reply.

* * * *

34

"Are you going to stay out here all night?" The professional tennis player, Michelle Minor had come, in her nightgown, to the sliding glass door out onto the corner balcony of the condo in the same Harbourside building on Shelter Cove that Charlotte and Brenda were in and spoken to her husband, the heartthrob movie actor and son of Brenda, Tony Trice. He was sitting in the dark, drinking, and watching the moonlight picking out the yachts rocking beside the piers of the marina. They were in a two-story condo, with the single bedroom above and the living/dining/kitchen spread below. The balcony wrapped around two sides of the condo.

"Until the music stops at Scott's," he answered, not taking his eyes off the muted activity on the boats in the marina. Scott's Fish Market Restaurant, which offered live music late into the night, was two floors directly below them. The music wasn't raucous this late at night.

"You've been quiet since dinner," Michelle said, picking the most nonconfrontational tone of voice she could manage. "I think you're upset about something. It was that film festival woman, Hannay Mongin, wasn't it?"

"Bingo. It's not like you didn't know she was flirting with you."

"Did you think I was flirting back?" Michelle asked. "Surely you're not that insecure with yourself. Have you looked at what the movie critics write about you and how sexy you are? They have you linked with every starlet you are seen with and do so brazenly, since we haven't publicly announced we're married. Since we're only known to be a steady couple, they titillate your fans with hints that you're still shopping. You think I'm shopping?"

"She's a woman."

"Tell your mother that, Tony. No, don't. I think you'd do irreparable harm to your healed relationship with her, if you did. You'd reveal you still haven't reconciled to that. To the point, since you bring it up, the tabloids have linked you to other male stars too. But while we're on the subject, I saw you look over at DeeDee Yance at that other table more than once. You didn't tell me that she would be here."

"I have no reservations about Mom's relationship with Charlotte. And as far as DeeDee in concerned, I didn't know she would be here. And she's married now."

"You wouldn't know it by the way she was looking at you," Michelle said. "But, guess what, I don't feel threatened by that. I'm going back upstairs. Suit yourself on when you come to bed. By the way, and not incidentally, have you talked to your aunt yet about what we'd like for her to do?"

"No, I haven't," he responded, a touch of belligerence in his voice. "She has a lot on her mind just now."

"I know she does, but perhaps you should think on why you haven't mentioned it to her," Michelle said before withdrawing from the doorway.

Ten minutes after she left, Tony's glass was empty. The bottle on the table wasn't, though. The music had stopped down at Scott's. He looked at the bottle and reached out for it. But then he said, "Fuck it." There were no answers to anything in that bottle. Who believed anything the *National Enquirer* published anyway? He knew there hadn't been anything between Michelle and that other female tennis player. The *Enquirer* was just trying to sell copies. He was being a chump. He rose from the table, and climbed the winding staircase to the bedroom. He was the luckiest man on earth; it was time for him to start showing he was.

* * * *

Otta rolled off to the side in the hotel bed. The sliding glass doors to the balcony facing the ocean were open, and, as her panting calmed, the sea breeze evaporated the thin film of sweat from her naked body. Both women lay there listening to the soothing sound of the surf as their hearts returned to a natural rhythm.

"That's an unusual name, Otta," Hannay Mongin murmured. "You say your family was from Savannah, but I know a Gullah woman on Daufuskie Island with that name. The Gullah's are from the original slaves brought over to the low country from Africa—many of them from Sierra Leone."

"I've heard references to Daufuskie in my family legends, but, yes, we're from Savannah. Otta is a long-handed-down family name. Stephens is from an old Hilton Head family. My people probably took the name of the family that once owned them. Your name is unusual too."

"Hannay is a Gullah name, popular on Daufuskie, from Sierra Leone as well, I think. Mongin is the family name of the one-time owners of one of the original plantations on Daufuskie, Oak Ridge. I've been told that the name Mungen Creek, which Daufuskie borders on is derived from the family name."

"Daufuskie itself is a funny name. It sounds Polish," Otta said.

"You pick a strange time to be asking geographic questions," Hannay said, "when I'm more interested in other forms of geographic exploration."

"It's the news reporter in me, I think," Otta paried. "I feel comfortable enough with you to exercise my natural curiosity."

"Well then, Miss Nosey, no, the island's name isn't Polish. It's pure Native American. It means 'sharp feather' in the Muscogee language. Apparently some ancient Muscogeen got the notion the island was shaped like a feather—like Hilton Head is shaped like a low-top boot. Various Native American groups have lived in the low country, including Daufuskie, for some nine thousand years. My people, the Gullah, were brought in during the eighteenth century because they knew how to work the rice and indigo fields."

"My family says we arrived here in the late eighteenth century too. Brought in as slaves. My people rather proudly say they weren't brought in as field hands, though, but as house slaves . . . and . . . the women to work in the brothels of Savannah."

"Thus the light skin coming down the generations," Hannay murmured.

"Yes, I guess so."

"Maybe your people were on Daufuskie at one time too. Otta is definitely a name I remember from the records I have from my ancestors."

"Yes, maybe," Otta said, not convinced.

"You should come over to Daufuskie someday," Hannay said. "My records are there. We should go through them to see if there are any connections. Somehow I feel connected to you."

Otta laughed. "We certainly were connected tonight." But then, more seriously, she said. "You have a place on Daufuskie?"

"Yes, a couple of old huts. They're small. Just one-room mud and shell-walled cottages, really—on the original Oak Ridge Plantation grounds—but they serve me well enough as retreats. They've been there for as long as our family history in South Carolina exists. They are almost on the beach. I can hear the surf as well there as we are doing from here."

"Yes, I think I'd like that," Otta said. She very much would like that, she thought to herself. And the woman claims to have family records going way back. Otta certainly would like to see those.

"We'll have to arrange a visit when I return from South America, then?"

"You'll be travelling abroad soon?" Otta asked.

"Yes, on business but only for a few days—before the film evening in Charleston with Brenda Brandon and before she does the film fundraiser in Savannah. I need to go use the bathroom," Hannay added, rolling away from Otta and sitting on the side of the bed. "I'm afraid you'll have to leave then. I would have liked for you to stay the night . . . but . . ."

"But you had planned to be somewhere else tonight?"

"Yes, actually. Does that displease you?"

"No, of course not. It's flattering that you had plans but were here with me instead. So, I should go," Otta said, sitting up on the other side of the bed.

When she heard the bathroom door click, Otta moved quickly around the hotel room. She was searching for that ivory bracelet she'd seen Hannay wearing at Bistro 17 and Pegg's bar. She hadn't seen where it had gone when the two of them were plastered to each other, pulling at each other's clothes before they fell into the hotel bed. She hadn't the presence of mind to keep the bracelet in sight then and she could kick herself for having let her libido control. But the woman was just too gorgeous and sexy—and willing. She didn't want to steal it; she just wanted to look at it and hold it for a minute.

She couldn't find it, though, and turned to picking up her clothes and putting them back on before Hannay came out of the bathroom and Otta left the room.

Otta hadn't found the bracelet, but Hannay had been more successful in her own hunt. When Otta had been in the bathroom earlier, Hannay had made her own search of Otta's purse and clothes. She had originally just wanted to verify who Otta was—that she had given her real name and really was a newspaper reporter. The name "Otta" had hit Hannay like a ton of bricks. The name, in fact, had many associations that came to Hannay's mind. Her surprise from looking through Otta's purse, though, was to have found the sketch of a bracelet identical to the one she wore that night. She didn't know what was up with that, but she made sure to hide the bracelet well before Otta came out of the bathroom.

Until Hannay could figure out what, other than a story on film festivals and a little girl-on-girl sex, Otta Stephens was up to, she'd have to keep the young woman close. Not everything Hannay was involved in was something she wanted to read about in the *Savannah Morning News*.

After Otta had left, Hannay dressed in travel clothes, packed, and checked out of the hotel. Craig Little, the shady character from Charlotte Diamond's past via Charlotte's younger brother and Charlotte's first husband, Sydney Morrison, was waiting for her in the Omni Oceanside Resort hotel lobby.

* * * *

DeeDee Yance, the movie star Brenda had worked with and new wife of the rock singer Trent Nichols woke, restless, at 3:00 a.m., in her bed in Nichols' Freeport Drive seaside mansion in the Haig Point golf club's gated community on the northeast edge of Daufuskie Island. Trent hadn't come to bed. There wasn't unusual for Trent. He roamed at night, often high on alcohol or drugs, and did his best composing of rock songs in that condition and at this hour. DeeDee often was wakened at night by the sounds of him composing downstairs in his music studio. That wasn't what wakened her tonight, though. What woke her was the sound of an airplane engine, close at hand, coming from the west, across Daufuskie itself rather than from the northeast where there was a small airport on Hilton Head Island. There was no airport on Daufuskie Island.

She woke with that thought in mind—that there was no airport on Daufuskie, so there should be the sound of very-low-flying aircraft nearby. You only reached it by boat. DeeDee, a Hollywood girl, didn't like the isolation of that. There had been so much she had had to tolerate since marrying Trent—on the rebound from Tony Trice, the young movie heartthrob having turned her advances down. Trent was a wild guy when he was drunk or drugged up, which was often and which was standard for the business he was in. When he was in this condition, he could be abrasive, bordering on the violent, in stark contrast from his grinning, "anything goes" loose persona in public. And he was secretive as well. She was never sure what he was up to. He had a group of men friends living here on the island, several of them connected to his band business, who he met down by the beach and drank and smoked with—and whispered with, stopping and changing the subject when she joined them.

And Trent had bodyguards—ex-Marines who looked, and most likely were, rough and ready. Why did Trent need this much personal protection—especially in a walled compound on an isolated island?

DeeDee was increasingly apprehensive of being isolated here on Daufuskie and of being subject to the changing whims and personality of her new husband. The unexpected and unnerving sound of the plane engine drew her out of bed and over to the balcony doors on the side of the bedroom facing the island. The noise sounded, strangely enough, to be coming from nearby, not over on the South Carolina low country mainland. And when she got to the window, she saw that a section of the golf course, inland from Trent's mansion, was lit up. She nearly was rocked on her heels when she saw the two-engine plane glide down, just about the tree line nearby and land somewhere close.

This was unreal. There was no airport on Daufuskie Island. Even more apprehensive now than ever before, she went back to bed, to restlessly toss and turn, waiting for Trent to come to bed. When he did, she'd ask him about there being no airport on Daufuskie but there having been a plane that landed nearby. The silence now in the wake of the noisy airplane engine was disconcerting. Always before when Trent was up late at night like this, he'd be composing music downstairs and she'd hear the same chords being played over and over again. Not tonight. Tonight was different. She went to sleep with the thought "Not tonight; tonight is different" going over and over in her mind—and Trent still not in bed.

Chapter Four: Getting on with It

"Cotton, indigo, and rice."

"Are you putting together a shopping list, Marilyn?" Charlotte asked, as she brought a plate of blueberry muffins out onto the balcony of their condo overlooking Shelter Cove. She could see that Chance and Marilyn were late having their breakfast. Chance was right behind her, carrying a pot of coffee. The marina was busy with the bustle of boat owners grooming their money pits.

"Marilyn was just telling me what her ancestors' plantation here grew in the late eighteenth century," Brenda said. She gave Charlotte a warning look. Charlotte had started the day in their bedroom voicing the hope that Marilyn was off her family history on Hilton Head kick, and Brenda had suggested that it was a defense mechanism from worrying about her medical condition.

"Have you located where your family's plantation was?" Brenda asked Marilyn, turning toward her.

"Oh, yes, it's where the Wexford Plantation section is now, further down the main road from where we are and on this side of the road. Chance drove me over there yesterday, trying to locate where my mother's house was. We found the street, but not the house. Wexford was a name that came later than when my family settled here. We were Baldwins."

"They are all palatial mansions over there now," Chance said. "We're looking at a couple of them today that are for sale . . . but I don't know."

"You don't want to move really fast on that idea, I don't think," Charlotte said, as she planted her bulk at a corner of a table that was really only big enough for three, as it was pushed up against the balcony railing. Brenda, sitting next to her, facing

42

the balcony, didn't kick her in the shin, but she did touch Charlotte's forearm with her fingers, enough to remind Charlotte they'd been over this before breakfast as well—that they should leave it to Chance to deal with Marilyn's sudden urge to move to Hilton Head from their very nice retirement home in Williamsburg, Virginia. Marilyn had been open about the desire to come back to her roots to die, which had disturbed Charlotte and Brenda as much as it did Chance, especially since Marilyn, the minister, had always been the down-to-earth practical one of the foursome. But only Charlotte thought that the direct confrontation approach was the way to bring Marilyn back to earth on this. Brenda had been applying the brakes to Charlotte's instincts. Chance was walking around in sort of a daze, unsure of how to approach any of it.

"So, you'll be looking at houses in the Wexford Plantation area today?" Brenda said. "What else are you planning for the day? I'll be out on the Harbor Town golf course with Michelle, practicing for the celebrity tournament this morning and then Aaron is taking me to Charleston to check out the film night venue."

"We'll be going to Charleston today too," Chance said. This was news to both Charlotte and Brenda—Charleston was ninety-five miles and a two-hour drive north from here. It wasn't possible to just go to Charleston from Hilton Head like you were going down to the corner for some milk. But before either of the women could answer, Marilyn continued on her family reverie.

"We're going to stop at the Zion Chapel of Ease Cemetery on our way," she said. "The first church on the island was built there and I have ancestors' graves to visit. I believe the family still has some plots there; I've told Chance I want to check that out."

This was getting to be too much morbidity for Charlotte and she was about to say something when Chance took it down to an even lower level.

"You can tell them why we're going to Charleston, Marilyn. They'll want to know."

"I saw Dr. Gillespie yesterday," Marilyn said. "She was my mother's doctor at the end, and I've come back to her because she was so good with Mother. She wants me to go into

43

the hospital for some tests. We're going to the Hollings Cancer Center in Charleston. They want me to stay the night. There will be some tests this evening and then again tomorrow morning before they can tell me more about . . ." Words failed her at that point and she couldn't go on. But she didn't have too, Brenda and Charlotte each took a hand.

"I'm sure it will be just fine," Charlotte said.

"Would you like us to be there with you?" Brenda asked. "We both, of course, would be happy to be there."

"No, not then . . . but thanks," Marilyn said. "But maybe later . . . if they want me to stay—and if they need to operate."

The women went silent. Something between a snort and a sob sounded behind them, with Chance stepping off the balcony and into the condo. The three women, holding hands, turned their attention to the activity on the sailboats and small yachts moored at the marina piers in Shelter Cove. For some reason the life in the marina seemed so much more vibrant now than it had been fifteen minutes earlier.

* * * *

Charlotte and Brenda waited around in the condo until Marilyn and Chance had repacked their suitcases and, promising to text the two women Marilyn's hospital room number and where Chance was staying, with a loose intention of Brenda and Chance having dinner together in Charleston that evening, they waived the couple good-bye. By then Michelle had arrived to go golfing and Charlotte said, somewhat cryptically, that she had something on for the morning as well.

"Tony isn't going golfing with us?" Brenda asked, masterfully keeping evidence from her voice of her concern for the relationship between her son and Michelle, who she loved as a daughter.

"He has a script to memorize and is staying in for most the day. The setup for this movie he's supposed to be in has been messy. He doesn't know whether it will start filming a month from now or a year from now. So, he's studying the script to keep from fretting about the production woes," Michelle said. She didn't mention that he wasn't particularly communicative that morning. He had come to bed the previous night, though, so conditions could have been worse.

"Did I see Marilyn and Chance leaving as I came down the walkway?" Michelle asked. "Tony did say he needed to talk to Marilyn."

Brenda dearly wanted to ask what Tony wanted to talk to Marilyn about—this wasn't the first mention that he wanted to see her—but she didn't want to come across as an intrusive mother. She just said, "They've decided to go up to Charleston for an overnight," and Michelle didn't pursue the point. Until Marilyn released her control over her news, Brenda felt bound not to mention it.

Charlotte waited for Brenda and Michelle to leave before she took off and then she stayed within Shelter Cover, walking around the small yacht basin to the amphitheater and turning off down the pathway between two of the condo buildings until she came to the Mediterranean Harbour Bar and Grill, which had an open-air section under the condo building above. She was the last one to arrive at the long table tucked into a corner at the back of the open-air section. A screen blocked it off from the covered passage in front of two other shops between the restaurant and the central amphitheater courtyard.

Unbeknownst to Charlotte, Otta Stephens, the *Savannah Morning News* reporter, who had been waiting in the shadows for Charlotte to exit her condo, had followed Charlotte around the yacht basin and found a place on the other side of the screen where she could listen in on the quite serious meeting Charlotte was attending.

"Ah, Charlotte," FBI chief agent Evan Worthington, who was standing at the end of the table, said, "Now that you're here we can begin. You know, of course, Margaret Fancel and her husband, Dave Burch, both of whom you're worked with before. And, of course, you know our mutual friend, Doug Dolan. But I'd like to introduce you to Steve McCall, the novelist. It's Steve's story that has brought us all together today. Have a seat and we'll begin."

* * * *

45

Brenda and Michelle picked up a fan club as soon as they stepped out of Tony's Mercedes roadster at the entrance of the Sea Pines Harbour Town golf club building. The fans and paparazzi hadn't gathered knowing that Brenda and Michelle were going to be there, but had gotten wind that the rock star, Trent Nichols, was practicing at the club today. That he and the movie star, DeeDee Yance, had recently been married and that the press hadn't managed much coverage of that added to the press interest in a Nichols and Yance sighting. Brenda and Michelle were rich gravy.

Seeing a legendary movie actress and a hot, high-profile female pro tennis player join up with the newlywed couple for a foursome round around the links only added to the frenzy.

It didn't help the foursome's concentration on the golf, though. Michelle and Trent managed with a bit of difficulty, both accustomed to being followed by a crowd. DeeDee was hopeless at golf and wasn't in the celebrity tournament anyway, so she didn't get irritated with the fan worship. In fact, she liked the attention she was getting from the crowd more than anything involved in golf.

Brenda was the one who was not enjoying the experience. She wanted to do well in the tournament but she hadn't played much golf in some time. She had no trouble handling fawning admirers, but trying to handle both chores was not helping the golf.

"This doesn't seem to be working for you," Trent told her as they moved from one green to the next tee.

"I really need the practice and the fans are distracting me too much," she admitted.

"I can solve that," he said.

"Oh, how?"

"Come over to Daufuskie for a couple of days. You can stay with DeeDee and me. We live on a private club golf course. No outsiders are allowed in. You can practice your swing and putting in piece. I was serious with my invitation last evening."

"I'm not alone. I have a wife—as DeeDee told you. We're here on vacation. I wouldn't want—"

"By all means bring her along. Come on over on Monday."

"If it really would not be an imposition."

"Certainly not. DeeDee was telling me last night that she'd really like to show our place off to you."

Well, that was a lot easier than I thought it would be, Brenda thought, as she teed up her ball on the third hole. Before she and Michelle had left Shelter Cove earlier Charlotte had reiterated that she'd really like to have a couple of days on Daufuskie Island. And now that would happen. Brenda still wondered what the hell that all was about, though.

* * * *

"But you can see for yourself that there's no airfield on Daufuskie Island," Dave Burch said, pushing the aerial photographs across the table for the novelist, Steve McCall, to look at. There were six around the table at the Mediterranean Harbour Bar and Grill on Shelter Cove, Evan Worthington, at the head; Charlotte Diamond, across from him; David Burch and Margaret Fancel, on one side; and Steve McCall and Douglas Dolan, at the other. All were leaning over the table and speaking in conspiratorial whispers that, however, did project across the screen at the side to Otta Stephens's recording device.

"Nonetheless, there have been nights when I've heard airplane motor noises from my island house in the Melrose on the Beach housing area and seen bright lights from the northern area of the island come on and go off quickly. It's definitely the sound of a small plane leaving or arriving. I'm sure that's how they are coming and going."

"From your house, here," David Burch countered, "the Hilton Head airport is in the direction you say you're hearing the noise. There isn't another airport or airstrip nearby except for the one at Savannah, to the south. We have the area covered on these aerial photographs."

"I can hear the airplane noise from the Hilton Head airport too—and see the glow of the runway lights in that direction, but those are constant and farther away. What I'm talking about now is closer to hand. It sounds like it's coming from directly north of my house, on the island."

"But these photos don't lie," Burch persisted.

"Let's hold that in abeyance for now and back up," Evan Worthington interjected. "Steve is the one who put us on to this. Tell us about the woman, Steve."

"I saw her on the island, at night, when I was out jogging. I like to jog the old roads on the sparsely populated south portion of the island at twilight. This young woman, black, beautiful, in disheveled clothes more suited to the city than an isolated island, suddenly burst out of the foliage at the side of the road. There was something familiar about her. She was babbling in a foreign language I couldn't identify at the time. I think now that it was Portuguese, however."

"How did you determine that?" Charlotte asked, speaking up for the first time.

"I'm coming to that," McCall said, and picked up the thread of his story again. "Well, I could see that she was all scratched up, like she'd been blindly flailing around in the brush. We weren't far from my house, so I managed to convey to her that she should come to my place and we'd sort out what her problem was. She was wild eyed, obviously frightened of something. I kept asking her if she'd been attacked or assaulted, but she couldn't understand me. I got her to my house and settled her on the porch, saying I'd go in and get her a glass of water. When I came back she was gone."

"And then you realized you'd seen her earlier, didn't you?" Evan prompted.

"Yes, I saw her a couple of months before that—in Rio de Janeiro. That's how I decided she must have tried to speak to me in Portuguese when I saw her on Daufuskie. And I should mention," he said, looking at David Burch and fingering one of the aerial photographs, "that when I encountered her on Daufuskie, it was the night after I heard an airplane arriving somewhere close by and the sky was lit up north of me. I was sitting, drinking, on my porch and I saw the light."

"Drinking?" David asked.

"Yes, drinking. Not drunk," Steve answered.

"Go on. Rio de Janeiro."

"I was there to pick up background for a novel I'm working on."

"Yes, and you saw the young woman again, after you saw her on the island?" Evan prompted.

"Yes. In a brothel in Savannah." McCall stopped there, clearly embarrassed. "I was picking up background material there too, for the novel. I don't go to brothels normally. I'm gay."

"That doesn't matter," Evan said. "Go on. The young woman."

"She was in the brothel. One of the girls. They were behind a wall of glass, and we were supposed to pick out the one we wanted. She saw me and I saw her, and we recognized each other instantly. That's how I'm sure it was the same young woman. We both knew we'd seen each other before, the last time on Daufuskie Island. I turned to the madam to note that was the woman I wanted—just to talk to, for my research and because I wanted to know then what she'd been doing on Daufuskie . . ."

"Yes, and then?" Evan goaded him on.

"Then, when I turned back, she was gone."

"That's where we come in," Evan took over the discussion. "This is a photo of the woman. Her names was Maria Silva, born in a village not far from Rio de Janeiro." He sent the photo around; it was of the naked body of a young woman, taken at the edge of the surf on a beach on Tybee, near Savannah. "She didn't drown. She was strangled. She was traced back to the brothel and a photo was put in the papers there. Steve, here, recognized it and reported having seen her in a Savannah—and also here in South Carolina. We ran her prints through Interpol, and that came up with a missing persons report on her, connected with three other young women. Her home village in Brazil was what provided the ongoing connection that brought the FBI into the case and hence interviewing Steve and bringing the rest of us here today."

"Her home village in Brazil was the connection? I don't see how that brings the Annapolis FBI office in on it, though." Margaret Fancel asked the question. She looked around at Charlotte, who had been her supervising agent in the FBI's Annapolis office and who had been silent up to this point. She could see that Charlotte wasn't acting surprised, so she evidently had been brought more up to speed already in this case.

"Yes. She was one of four young woman of that village who had been caught up in prostitution. The other three had also wound up here in the United States—two in New York and one in Baltimore—but from what we can now gather, they came into the States somewhere around here—Savannah or Charleston. Two of those women are dead; the other two disappeared off the radar before we could pin them down. The other one who died was killed in Baltimore. That's what brought the Annapolis office into this. New York let us take the lead once we'd made a connection to Brazil and had an actual felony case to pursue."

"Entry at Savannah or Charleston or right here on Daufuskie Island and then moved on," Charlotte spoke up.

"Yes, because of what Steve has told us about Maria Silva, we believe the arrival spot is right here, near us."

"So, we want to get established on Daufuskie Island to observe and to track down Steve's mystery of the nearby air operations."

"Right," Evan said. "It's always a possibility that the women are entering the States in Savannah or Charleston and being boated here for some reason. But we can't discount that they are coming directly in here by air. So, we need to blanket the island with eyes. Steve has agreed to go back to his island house and work on his novel there, while maintaining observation of island activity and contact with us. We've rented a small house on School Road nearly in the center of the island for David and Margaret to continue their honeymoon there. Doug will be providing boat transportation for us all. And Charlotte?" He turned his gaze to Charlotte at the other end of the table.

"I'm working on that. Brenda has a tentative invitation from the musician, Trent Nichols, to spend a few days at his Daufuskie home. She's golfing with him at Harbour Town today, and I'm hoping he will make the invitation more definite."

"Good then," Evan concluded. "When everyone is in place, I'll be with Doug on his boat. Let's see if we can get this pinned down and solved within a couple of days. Let's get this sex slavery ring inside the United States preying on Brazilian woman shut down."

As they were dispersing, Otta Stephens shut off her recorder and disappeared back onto the promenade ringing the Shelter Cove yacht basin.

Douglas Dolan came to Charlotte and asked about Brenda. Charlotte could tell that he still held the torch for her glamorous spouse.

"She's golfing today. Going up to Charleston for the evening with Aaron Woolridge. She's checking out the Scottile Theatre at the College of Charleston, where they will be doing a film night."

"Do you think she'd mind if, after I've boated the Burches over to Daufuskie, I sailed up to Charleston and asked her to dinner."

"No, Doug, I think she'd enjoy that. Maybe she'll need transportation back to Hilton Head tonight."

Dolan beamed at the permission given. Charlotte gave the permission completely secure in her relationship with Brenda—and feeling a bit sorry for Douglas Dolan. Of course, he could just join a long line of men pining for the attention of the movie star. They didn't have a clue what satisfied the woman. It surprised the hell out of Charlotte that it apparently was her.

* * * *

"You can assure me that Ana is no longer pregnant and is well enough to travel?"

"Yes, of course," Herman Garcia, a major Brazilian manufacturer assured Hannay Mongin. They were sitting across from each other on sofas in front of a two-story glass wall overlooking the exclusive Urca neighborhood of Rio de Janeiro. They were in a penthouse apartment at the top of a modern building. Craig Little was sitting off to the side and behind Hannay. The young woman in question, Ana Fernandez, the Garcias's erstwhile nanny, was standing in a doorway to a kitchen, her eyes cast down, dressed in a demur suit, which didn't hide the voluptuous curves of the young woman's body. A suitcase was standing on end beside her.

The new nanny, a much older—and plainer—woman was upstairs with the children. Mrs. Garcia had gone to a spa for the day, instructing her husband to have done with it all before she came home—or to pack and leave before she returned. The pretty Ana had been irresistible and Herman Garcia had not resisted.

Mr. Garcia had bought Ana travel clothes and given her a large sum of money—in terms of what Ana would think was a large sum—so, although apprehensive, she wasn't fearful. He wouldn't have given her money and arranged for this American woman to help her if any harm was going to come to her. And Miss Mongin and her chauffer were, indeed, nice to her as they took her to lunch and then to Miss Mongin's hotel to wait for the flight they were going to take her on. That's where the "nice" ended, though. The chauffer, who Miss Mongin called Craig, slapped her around, pulling her clothes off her. Then he put her on the bed and did to her what Mr. Garcia had done—repeatedly—over the previous three months, until he had gotten her with child.

Miss Mongin sat in a chair and watched. When the man was finished, Miss Mongin "comforted" her. Ana watched helplessly, with the woman on top of her, as Craig went through Ana's purse and suitcase and took the money Mr. Garcia had given her.

Craig held Ana down then, while Miss Mongin gave Ana drugs with a syringe that made the young woman drowsy and unable to control her arms and legs. The tied her up, put her in the closet, and then left the room.

From the hotel Hannay and Craig went to the Copacabana area of the city, to a club named Sexdesejo, where a club manager had contacted Hannay and said one of his girls, Julia, was giving him trouble and he wanted to be rid of her. Hannay and Craig watched the girl perform on stage, went backstage then and paid for some time with her in one of the rooms in the back. And then, while Craig kept her occupied, Hannay shot Julia up with the drowsing drug.

Both young women were awake but docile and needing help walking when Craig drove them and Hannay out to the airport and to his Sukhoi Su-80 short take-off and landing aircraft, which had been guarded through the afternoon by a former mercenary soldier in Afghanistan and a current professional bodyguard named Butch, who also was a certified copilot. The airport authorities had been well paid to forget that the aircraft had ever been there that day. Within minutes of loading the two drowsy young women into the plane, to join another drugged young Brazilian woman named Lara, it was up in the air and on its way north. The plane would make one, undocumented, well-compensated stop in Guyana for refueling between Rio and its final destination.

Chapter Five: Saturday Night

Later that Night

Charlotte and Evan ate a quiet dinner with Tony and Michelle at Ela's on the Water in the harbor master's building at the Broad River entrance to Shelter Cover. The Restaurant was at the opposite end of the marina from the Harbourside 1 condo building where most of them were staying. None of them spoke of what was on their minds—relationships and, in Charlotte and Evan's case, the sex slave case they were both working on, each invigorated by working with the other again.

They spoke of Marilyn and Chance and of Marilyn's medical concern, which was a concern for all of them, and of Brenda and the possibility of appearing in the movie director Aaron Woolridge's pirate movie. And they spoke of Tony's own coming movie and how he was having difficulty focusing on learning his lines. Luckily, it had been cast and the scripts produced almost a year before filming started. Tony was a fast study. In many ways Michelle believed he was using the need to memorize lines as an excuse for them not talking out their marital difficulties.

They spoke also of the charity golf tournament and of the volatile rock star, Trent Nichols, who was now in a foursome for the tournament with Michelle and Brenda and a pro golfer. The latter was all business, and the only one he was giving respect in the foursome was Michelle, because she at least was as a professional athlete and one whose name he knew.

They walked back to Harbourside 1 after dinner, and Tony and Michelle went directly up to their condo. Meanwhile Charlotte and Evan lingered on the walkway at the water's edge that was sunk a little lower than the first-floor covered passage under the condos, the first floors of the Harbourside condos being given over to shops and restaurants. The music was still going at Scott's Fish Market Restaurant, and Charlotte sat on a bench, facing the yacht piers and listening to the music.

In the condo Tony grabbed a beer and went out on the balcony to watch the night activity in the boats in the yacht basin. He saw that Charlotte and Evan were sitting on a bench down by the water and deep in conversation. Michelle, in a nightgown and robe, came out on the balcony, put her arms around her husband from the back, and rested her chin on his shoulder.

"It's OK for you to be worried about Marilyn," she said, thinking that his deepening moodiness was about something else altogether, though—something between the two of them.

"Yes, of course," he responded. But, realizing that his response had been abrupt and sharper than her question merited, he revealed another element of what had him up tight. "It's this movie too. My role is a tortured soul one. I can't help but take on some of the character's moodiness if I'm going to play the role well."

"Understood," Michelle said, glad to have that out—she'd known he was tied up in a difficult movie role—but knowing that wasn't all, knowing that he was brooding about more than that. She couldn't resist adding, though, "But the movie is nearly a year off for filming. Can't you establish character in a few months? Do you have to go for a year in the role without playing it?" He just snorted at that and she shut up, already feeling she'd gone over the "nag" line.

"And Charlotte and Evan," Tony said, gesturing to the two sitting on the bench below the balcony. "He's come back into her life. Look at them. They no doubt are talking about old times—times they have had together and not just the professional ones. I worry about Mother and Charlotte . . . how strong their relationship is. I don't want either one of them to be hurt. Douglas Dolan was there, in the restaurant, at dinner last night too. I know that Mother tried not to notice him, but she couldn't resist looking over at him. Charlotte and Brenda are here with different purposes. Mother has so many activities and so many people pulling at her. Charlotte is just in the background here. She may be vulnerable to Evan, just as Brenda could be vulnerable to Douglas Dolan. Charlotte and Evan are down there, no doubt talking about when they were together, and maybe with Charlotte regretting a decision to go with someone as public and busy as my mother."

"I think they are strong enough to withstand all temptation," Michelle said.

"Maybe. But you know how people talk, and the relationship between Mother and Charlotte is one not everyone accepts and one they are quick to gossip about."

"Like the life of a pro tennis player, don't you think?" Michelle said. He'd given her an opening. They had to face this sometime.

"I suppose."

"There doesn't have to be a hint of truth in an article like the one that appeared in the *National Enquirer*, Tony. You know that. There are fake articles linking you with women—and sometimes even men—all of the time. That doesn't mean that I believe any of it or that you need to worry about whether there's a grain of truth in it. Truth isn't part of the formula of a *National Enquirer* article."

"Yes, I guess that's true," Tony said. And thinking back to the fall, when the *National Enquirer* had him linked with a male pro basketball player just because Tony went to a couple of the guy's games. He had to admit, if begrudgingly, that there was no reason to doubt Michelle.

"The mood you've been in doesn't have anything to do with finding DeeDee here, does it?" she asked, deciding that, now that they were having this discussion, they might as well get it all out.

"DeeDee Yance? No, what would that have to do with anything?" She took his response as totally genuine. He hadn't been thinking of his former girlfriend.

"The *National Enquirer* makes it all up," Michelle said. "You and DeeDee were once a real item, and I never thought she gave you up easily. I don't think there's anything sparking between you two either, but it's a more real possibility than me making imaginary time with another woman, according to the *Enquirer*, don't you think?"

"Yes, you're right," he said, cracking a smile for the first time in days. "It's all just silliness."

Again, Michelle took Tony's response as genuine. "Come, let's go to bed," she said.

"OK," he answered, turning and following her into the condo, with one last, concerned look down to where Charlotte and Evan were sitting on the bench. Was it his imagination, or were they sitting closer together now than they had been earlier?

If he'd known what Charlotte and Evan were really talking about, it would have surprised the hell out of him.

They had come closer to each other on the bench because Evan had aerial shots of Daufuskie Island that he and Charlotte were looking at together, trying to figure out how a plane could be landing on the island. The whole time they'd been sitting on the bench, they'd been going over the sex slave ring case.

"We have to do something fast," Evan said. "Not just because bringing in undocumented aliens to work in the sex industry here is something we need to stop, but also because young women are dying. There have been two deaths that we know of so far and we've just started on the case."

"I have to think that we've narrowed down where it centers to this area, Evan," Charlotte said. "We're pretty far along. When we all get into place on the island Monday, I have to think that something will break loose."

"You're not going over until Monday? Not tomorrow?"

"Brenda has called from Charleston. They want to do an exploratory operation on Marilyn tomorrow at the Hollings Cancer Center. Brenda's coming back here later tonight, but we're both returning to Charleston tomorrow to be with Chance during the operation."

"So, Brenda's not upstairs already?"

"She won't be back for hours. But I should go up now."

"Would you like me to come up—for a nightcap?"

"I'm tired. And any more booze and I won't be able to get to sleep. I'll say goodnight here. Doug will have his boat here in the Shelter Cove marina to take us to the island Monday morning?"

"Yes, of course. I'll see you then." The both stood, had a moment of awkwardness, and then hugged before they went their separate ways. If Evan had been making a pass, she had

57

gotten beyond the offer without giving a hint she understood it as a pass. Maybe she didn't take it that way. And maybe Evan didn't mean it that way either.

Maybe.

* * * *

Brenda had been delighted to get the call from Douglas Dolan suggesting that he meet her for dinner in Charleston on Saturday night. She had just been with Marilyn and Chance at the cancer center where Marilyn had gotten the news that there was enough evidence of something in her breast from the earlier tests that they needed to operate and determine what it was.

"Don't be alarmed yet," Dr. Gillespie had said. "Most often it's just a cyst and we can take carry of that quickly and without anything serious being involved."

Marilyn took the news well, almost relieved that something was going to be done about the issue quickly, and grateful that they could operate the next day, on a Sunday. Still, it had been a strain on all three of them to find that something needed to be done.

Earlier in the day, in the first of two rattling revelations, Brenda had been with Aaron Woolridge and his new wife, the actress Cheryl Chandler, at the Scottie Theatre in the College of Charleston complex, where Brenda had performed at the annual Spoleto performance arts festival five years earlier and where she and Charlotte had been taken up in an FBI terrorism case. Hannay Mongin, who Brenda had met the evening before on Hilton Head and who was the executive director of the attempt to revive the Charleston Film Festival, had been scheduled to meet Brenda here and go over the film night the actress was to speak at, but the woman had been called out of town unexpectedly, so Aaron Woolridge was doing the honors. While Aaron was showing Brenda around the theater and discussing the film night to come, she couldn't help thinking about that and how the Spoleto case had brought her and Charlotte ever closer as a couple.

The two films they were showing for Brenda to discuss in Charleston were two that had loomed large in Brenda's life and had been just as important in her forming relationship at the time with Charlotte. Brenda didn't know how much she could share with an audience—that she could bear to share with them—about those two movies. The filming of *Woman Scorned* when Brenda was flying high in Hollywood became a crime case of note when her partner at the time, the costume designer Helga Lund, had been murdered—swinging from a chandelier in the couple's two-story foyer—in the same way Brenda's character had murdered her lover in the film. This automatically had cast suspicion on Brenda and had driven her out of Hollywood and to her childhood home in Hopewell, Maryland, where she had met the retired FBI agent, Charlotte Diamond, on the rebound from a marriage that had gone bad, and their relationship had begun, starting with Charlotte clearing Brenda's name of the death of Helga Lund.

The second movie, *White Orchid Found*, filmed in the Florida Everglades two years later, was memorable in that it involved another murder mystery, solved yet again by Charlotte, and had both advanced her relationship with Charlotte and included the painful public revelation that one of the young male actors in the film, Tony Trice, was Brenda's lovechild, born before she came to Hollywood and followed and nurtured by her from afar until he too had become a movie actor. It was during the filming of that movie as well that DeeDee Yance, a supporting actress in the film, had, to Brenda's dismay, started putting her claws into Tony.

Thank goodness Tony had gotten over DeeDee, Brenda thought, but it worried her that DeeDee had shown up in Hilton Head again when Tony was here and having some difficulties with his wife, Michelle Minor, who Brenda liked tremendously.

What could she tell audiences about the filming of either of these movies without being dragged down into revelations about her life and relationships that she didn't want to reveal to the public? It didn't help, as Aaron took her around the Scottile Theatre and discussed the film night to come, that his wife was there, trailing behind them, her vengeful eyes boring into Brenda's back. Cheryl Chandler, who had worked her way into Aaron Woolridge films as Brenda was trying to work her way out and had taken over the roles Brenda previously had played, strutted around this evening, acting like the cat who had swallowed the canary. Brenda had found out why.

"Have you had time to look over the script of the pirate movie?" Aaron had asked.

"Yes. The part looks like it would be both fun and challenging to play," Brenda answered. She was speaking of the part of the governor's wife, who was abducted by the pirate king.

"I think you'll be perfect as the governor's mother," Aaron said, completely innocent and oblivious to how this would age Brenda in the movie. "It's an award-welcoming character role. Cheryl will, of course, play the governor's wife."

"Of course," Brenda responded, only her great talent as an actress enabling her not to scream in frustration. Not only had she never thought of herself in wise and wise-cracking matron roles, even though she now was of that age, but she also didn't think of herself as a generation older than Cheryl Chandler. Cheryl was not more than ten years younger than Brenda, and although pretty, was never hailed as a world-class beauty as Brenda still was. The only upside to any of this was that Cheryl looked absolutely deflated that Brenda hadn't had a tantrum over the casting.

"It's a pity that we'll have to have your legendary blonde hair dyed gray, though. We'll go with a gray that evokes the platinum blonde or your fans will be disappointed." Aaron was prattling on, completely unaware that he had introduced leveling revelations Brenda hadn't absorbed until then. If she'd known she'd slipped into the type of role he was offering, she probably wouldn't accept any more movie roles. He was an old friend and a long-time colleague, though—and he had no idea how he had devastated her. She'd do this one more time—just for him, and in spite of Cheryl Chandler. The irony right at this moment was that she alone knew that she wouldn't have to dye her legendary hair to achieve gray. Perhaps, she thought, that should have alerted her to the reality she had been ignoring.

She'd already agreed to have dinner with Chance and now she couldn't turn down an offer to dine with Aaron and Cheryl as well or Cheryl would have known how deflated Brenda was, so when Douglas Dolan, a one-time flame of hers, called about dinner as well, Brenda leaped at the chance to balance

Chance's worry and despondency with the Woolridges's totally disconnected isolation of Brenda from her place in the movie world as she had been fantasizing it had remained even as she had been withdrawing from it.

"Shall I make reservations at the Peninsula Grill? For seven o'clock?" she asked Doug over the phone. "They always make room for me there. There would be five of us."

"Five of us?" Doug asked, surprised and disappointed. He'd wanted her all to himself.

"Yes. I've already made a date with Chance Diamond and Aaron and Cheryl Woolridge."

"That would be great," Doug answered cheerily, feeling anything but cheery. "And after dinner, how about I bring you back to Shelter Cove on my boat? Charlotte said it was unclear how you were going to get back to Hilton Head tonight."

"That would be great too," she answered. And Doug thought that was going to be as great as he could get out of this. They'd be alone on the water for hours. He would do whatever he possibly could do in rekindling what they once almost had.

Dinner went well, Brenda delighted that she had someone to talk to other than an understandably distracted Chance and a catty Cheryl. Rekindling any sort of romance with Doug later didn't happen in her mind, though. Throughout the sail from Charleston to Hilton Head, Brenda had nothing she wanted to talk about more than how happy she and Charlotte were together and all of the adventures they had fallen into and both survived and thrived on since they had met. A suggestion that they heave to in Beaufort en route and break out champagne he had on ice to celebrate didn't go anywhere when Brenda, quite honestly, said she wasn't in a celebratory mood and was anxious to get back to Hilton Head and Charlotte.

The best he got was a brushed kiss touching his lips and then his cheek, a hurried thanks, and a tinkling laugh in the Shelter Cove yacht basin as she hopped out of the boat and scurried up the pier toward the Harbourside 1 condo and Charlotte, waiting for her, in bed, unable to sleep until Brenda was safely home again.

* * * *

Steve McCall, sitting on the porch of his Daufuskie Island Aprils' Way house, facing the entrance into the Calibogue Sound from the Atlantic Ocean, was having trouble concentrating on his writing. He felt isolated and vulnerable. There were times when he was sorry he had reported seeing the young Brazilian woman here and at the brothels. It was good material to put into his novel and it had become key to the book, but then he became afraid that, if there was a big sex slave ring behind all of this, someone might read his book, figure out he had seen something he shouldn't have, and come after him. That was the real reason he'd reported it to the FBI.

No, it isn't. He was haunted by the look of panic on the young woman's face when she stumbled out of the brush on School Road and tried to beg him for help. He had kept playing the encounter over and over in his mind. What had he done to spook her again when he'd brought her back to the house? Why had she bolted again? What had happened that made her wind up in those brothels—and then dead? And was she dead because he'd seen her there?

Was he in danger too, even now? The feds would all be here by Monday. The young couple, the Burches, should be set up in the Evans Cottage over on School Road already. He'd been told not to have contact with them—not to do anything suspicious or that would bring suspicion on them. He wondered if they really were over there. He could go out for his run and check that out. He hadn't run yet this evening. Of course, it no longer was evening. It was after ten. But there was no reason he couldn't go out for a run. There would be nothing unusual in that. He could run past Evans Cottage over on School Road— just to see if there were lights on, if the Burches were really there.

He'd feel a lot safer if he knew he wasn't the only one on the island who knew about the feds' operation. He certainly wasn't getting any work done.

He'd go for a run, see that he wasn't alone here, and come back and try to finish up the draft of this chapter. He'd done 450 words. He read that his favorite author, Graham Greene, made himself write 500 new words every day. That wasn't much. Steve usually did far more than that. He only had 450 words today, though. He'd go out for a run and then come back and finish that off.

He got over onto School Road, when he saw the sky light up off to the north, not very far, and still on the island. He'd told them at the meeting at Shelter Cove about the light and that it was on the island. He wasn't the far from Evans Cottage. He'd go there and . . . but, no, wait. He'd been told not to make direct contact.

As he stood there, on School Road, a funny-looking twin-engine airplane swooped down from out of the sky and went below the treetops just to the north of where he was standing. Melrose on the Beach, the community he lived in, was off to the east of where he stood. What was to the north was the exclusive, gated Haig's Point Golf Club community. The plane had come down somewhere there. It wasn't far. He'd jog over there, find out what was really what with that airplane—he'd told them at the Shelter Cove meeting that a plane was landing and taking off from Daufuskie—and then he'd come back and call over to Hilton Head. He'd been given a telephone number, but he hadn't brought it with him.

He jogged north on School Road, took at left on Turtle Beach Road when School dead ended, and then hung a right on Haig Point Road toward the gated club. He kept an eye on the lights. They really were strong and covered quite an area, but they flashed off soon after the plane had come down. He got to the wall of the golf club property. He was somewhere near the far end of the golf club's fairways. The ritzy vacation mansions of the super wealthy were to the northeast of here on the banks of the Calibogue Sound.

The wall wasn't all that high. He had no trouble getting over it. He came down near a fairway. He couldn't see where either the tee or the hole were. What he could see, though, was where two steel poles, with fake tree branches at the top, were hiding banks of lights. He was moving over to one of those, when he heard the dogs. He turned to climb back over the wall. He knew enough already to locate the feds when they arrived.

He didn't hear the shot.

The Burches, in Evans Cottage, on School Street, did hear the shot. They hadn't seen the sky light up or heard the sound of airplane engines nearby, even though their cottage was a tiny, 500-square feet one, because they were, after all, on a gifted honeymoon. They had been in the shower together, with the CD player on full blast to provide appropriate background music. They did get out of the shower and turned the volume down in time to hear the report of gunshot something to the north of them.

"Did you hear that?" Margaret had said.

"Yes. A gunshot," David answered. "This is pretty much a private island without hunting laws. They see something moving at night they don't like, they probably just shoot it."

David Burch had no appreciation for just how true those words were.

* * * *

Otta Stephens was sitting at the bar at Pegg's on Dunnagans Alley near midnight, stirring her Margarita with a swizzle stick and contemplating what she had heard earlier that day at Shelter Cover and considering what she would do with it. It was too explosive to just write it up and send it into the newspaper. But she could contact this Evan Worthington guy—or maybe Charlotte Diamond; they seemed to be senior in this—and parley what she already knew into an exclusive when their operation went down. At least she thought she should be able to. The Savannah media didn't do all that much business with the FBI. Every time she got euphoric about the scope she might have, she had misgivings about being out of her league with anything dealing with the FBI. When she had that thought, she took a swig of her Margarita, which was probably more than one reason why she was a little spaced out and she was getting the attention she was in Pegg's.

More than one woman had approached her at the bar and tried to strike up a conversation, but Otta wasn't there to attract just any woman. She wasn't all that sure on a conscious level why she'd come back to Pegg's to contemplate the ticking bomb she'd gotten a hand on, but subconsciously she knew why.

She'd spent the afternoon and a good part of the evening transcribing what she'd recorded. The voices had been muffled and were purposely muted, so it hadn't been easy to hear, but she thought she'd figured it all out. She took some notes then and did some Internet research. This could really be explosive. It was explosive enough that she'd put everything in a copy, packing, and mailing facility lock box before coming over to unwind at the bar. She wouldn't want anyone to find that material in her hotel room or car. She'd need to figure out a way to get over to Daufuskie Island. That hot woman the previous night—the one she'd met here in this bar, Hannay Mongin, had invited her over to the island. She'd been interested in the Mongin woman for different reasons than this, but if she could hook up with her again, which was why, she subconsciously knew, Otta had come back to this bar . . .

And then, as if by magic, there she was, perching on the stool beside Otta.

"Hi," she said. "I hoped I'd find you here."

"Hi yourself," Otta answered. "I thought you said you had to go on a trip."

"I did," Hannay Mongin answered. "It was a day trip. I'm back . . . and thirsty . . . and restless."

"Sounds good to me," Otta said. "Didn't you invite me to come over to Daufuskie—that you had some family genealogy to show me?"

"Yeah. You want to come over and spend a couple of days with me at my cottage there?"

"That would be great."

"I don't know if I can hold my need long enough to go over there tonight, though," Hannay said. "Do you have someplace we can go tonight and I'll take you over there tomorrow? I gave up my room at the Omni."

"I have a room at the Red Roof Inn on the Regency Parkway. It's cheap—for Hilton Head. But it's got a bed and a shower."

"Perfect," Hannay said, with a big smile. "Just what the doctor ordered."

That was perfect with Otta too. She hadn't come to any resolutions on what to do with the FBI operation information she'd gathered, and working on the "Hannay Mongin and the ivory bracelet" issue would permit her to put the other matter on hold. Regardless, she could work on both if she could get an excuse to be on Daufuskie Island.

Chapter Six: Not So Quiet Sunday

It was a sleepy and reticent group of Charlotte, Brenda, Michelle, and Troy who drove up together to Charleston early on Sunday morning to give Chance Diamond support while Marilyn was in surgery at the Hollings Cancer Center. They got there before Marilyn was wheeled into the operating room, where she did her ministerial best to give them comfort and was obviously pleased they had all come. They went to a waiting room to sweat it out.

Brenda paced around the waiting room, while Charlotte and Michelle kept Chance talking and as distracted as they could and Tony worked on memorizing his lines for his coming movie. Brenda was observing everyone and everything, so she was the one who noticed that hospital personnel kept looking in—at either Brenda, Tony, or Michelle, recognizing them and buzzing to each other about the celebrities in the waiting room. After a bit of this, she could take no more. The next time a nurse looked in, Brenda asked her if she could talk with the hospital administrator.

She could—and within a half hour, Brenda, Tony, and Michelle were making the rounds of the hospital rooms and nursing stations and greeting and encouraging—and giving a thrill—to all at the center that day.

This left Charlotte and Chance alone in the waiting room for a while, and the sister and brother had a heart-to-heart conversation.

"I'm sure she'll be fine, Chance," Charlotte said for the twentieth time. "She's a tough lady and her profession and the way she's gone about it put her on the winning side."

Chance was a doctor. He held no illusions about just being on the side of the almighty as protection against anything. He certainly didn't think Charlotte believed all of that. But he appreciated his sister giving it a try. Seeing that this didn't give him false hope, Charlotte decided to retreat to what had been concerning her. "Did you and Marilyn find any likely houses in Wexford Plantation when you were house hunting?"

"Nothing we liked any better than where we live in Williamsburg. But Marilyn asked the Realtor to dig up some more possibilities."

"You know you won't find anything as nice in Wexford as you have in Ford's Colony. The pricing just isn't comparable."

"You know that and I know that, but Marilyn doesn't want to accept it. This cancer scare has sent her back to her heritage. And if that's how she wants to play it . . ."

"Yes, yes, of course," Charlotte said. In the silence, Chance abruptly stood.

"They said it would be more than an hour yet. I think I'll go for a walk."

"That sounds like a good idea," Charlotte said. "They have a beautiful garden here. Why don't you go check that out? I'll stay here. If there's any news, I'll come get you."

When Charlotte was alone, she pulled the aerial photos of Daufuskie Island out of her briefcase and started going over then again, looking at them from every angle and considering every possibility. Michelle came back to the waiting room before the others, and Charlotte called her over.

"You're the golfer, Michelle. And God certainly knows I'm not. I don't know much about the game, but I've always heard of golf games being played in nine or eighteen holes."

"That's right," Michelle said.

"So, a golf club would have nine or eighteen holes or some combination of that?"

"Normally, yes. I don't know of any courses with a different setup."

"So, why do you think that this golf course on Daufuskie Island—the Haig Point Club—has nineteen fairways? Here, take a look at this photo."

Michelle took the photo and counted the fairways. "I can't think of any reason they would—and this fairway, this one here, look, is a whole lot longer than the others. And it's absolutely straight and has no sand traps. I don't even see a green. The other fairways on the photo have both."

"Thanks. That's what was bothering me," Charlotte said. She took her cellphone out and called Evan, who she presumed was back on Hilton Head, on Doug Dolan's yacht, finalizing operational plans for the assault on Daufuskie Island.

"I think I've found how there can be a landing strip on Daufuskie Island," she said, and she went on to tell him about the added fairway at the Haig Point Club. "It looks like Steve McCall had the right call on that."

"Good girl," Evan replied. "We'll have to give McCall praise for sticking to his guns on that when we see him tomorrow."

"What's that noise in the background, Evan? Do you and Doug have dancing girls on his boat with you?"

"No, I'm in a brothel," Evan said. And then he laughed.

"I'll tell you about it when we're together next. Gotta go now." And he clicked off on his cellphone.

Charlotte might have called him back, but Marilyn's doctor appeared in the waiting room doorway then, still in his scrubs, and was asking for Chance. Charlotte went to get him and Michelle went forth to round up Brenda and Tony.

The news was good. Everything was benign and everything was taken care of. Relief and congratulations abounded. All stayed around to visit with Marilyn before she was tucked away for the night with the promise she would be released to Chance and could return to her Hilton Head vacation the next day.

"Chance, Mom, Charlotte, would it be OK if I spoke to Marilyn alone for a minute before we leave?" Tony asked.

Of course it was OK, and he came out of the room beaming. The beaming continued among the foursome who had been so introspective and sad that morning when they returned to Hilton Head late that afternoon, all smiles and chatter and everything being right with the world. It was the time to think about launching an assault on Daufuskie Island the next day— and only Charlotte, of the four, was fully aware of that danger that loomed ahead there.

* * * *

Evan Worthington and Douglas Dolan had been close friends from years before when Brenda and Charlotte had been planning and building the movie folks retirement home, Curtain Call, in Hopewell on the Choptank, and the two men had been wooing Charlotte and Brenda, respectively, and thus doing a lot of double dating. Evan, the new FBI agent in charge in Annapolis and an old flame of Charlotte's, was trying at the time to get Charlotte back with the FBI as a consultant and back in his bed, succeeding only in the first. Doug, a St. Michael's, Maryland, based architect, helping to build Curtain Call, had been smitten immediately by Brenda, who had warmed to him as well. Both men amicably gave way to Charlotte's and Brenda's attraction to each other and remained friends. Since Doug had a small cabin cruiser he virtually lived on and Evan saw the need for water transportation in an operation targeting an island accessible only by boat, Evan had brought his friend down to Hilton Head to help out. Doug was happy to be included, especially since Brenda would be there.

Doug's boat was moored in the Shelter Cove marina and aboard this vessel was where Doug and Evan had found themselves late Saturday night, sharing beer and wounded pride at each having made some form of pitch that evening to the woman he had pursued and lost back in the Curtain Call construction period, and happy to commiserate with each other. The two had spent the night on the boat, when Evan got the call Sunday morning from Shirley Elgin, another old flame of his, who now was the FBI agent in charge in Savannah. Evan, Shirley, and Charlotte had all been together in basic agent training at Quantico, Virginia. Evan and Shirley had been a number until Charlotte arrived, and then Evan went for Charlotte instead. They all eventually went their own ways in separate assignments, with Evan marrying yet a different woman, Ruth. Ruth had died a few years back, but Shirley had never lost the torch for Evan or resentment of Charlotte, who had not been aware that there was a Shirley when she succumbed to Evan's charms. Shirley now contacted Evan to let him know she had tracked down a few women in Savannah he might want to interview in his current case, Doug was quite willing to take him to Savannah by boat.

The women in question, one originally from Brazil and the other from Colombia, had been panicked by the murder of Maria Silva and, having gotten to the States the same way she had and for the same ultimate purpose, were suddenly willing to talk to the authorities about their own journeys. Shirley Elgin, who was still carrying a flame for Evan and was ever hopeful, had busted a gut to track the women down, to break down their resolve to keep their stories to themselves, and to prepare them to be willing to talk to Evan.

Shirley was so anxious to be accommodating to Evan that she arranged a mooring for Doug's boat at the River Street front, where the tourist boats usually reigned. Leaving Doug there to mind his yacht, she whisked Evan away for a visit to two brothels, including the exclusive Tisdale Club, and a burlesque house. Rattled by the death of Maria Silva and the cajoling and promise of protection by Shirley Elgin, two of the women were willing to relate similar stories about being transported to the States and, ultimately, their current jobs via South Carolina. They didn't know it was Daufuskie Island, but they described it well enough for it to be a good possibility. They also both said they were recruited by a beautiful, young black woman. One of the women was fully willing to enter the States illegally; the other one was tricked into it but had become satisfied with her lot here rather than where she came from.

Something was ringing a bell with Evan on the woman bringing the sex workers to the States. One of the prostitutes told Evan the woman said her family had come to the States as slaves and that she lived where the plane landed, somewhere near enough to Savannah that it didn't take long for the women to be brought there—by boat. That tended to confirm that they'd arrived via Daufuskie Island, and this was further pinned down when Charlotte called him with the solution to the mystery of a plane landing on an island with no airstrip: it was landing on what looked like a golf course fairway.

What finally clicked with Evan was that the prostitutes described a woman identical to Hannay Mongin, who Evan had heard at dinner the other night in a Shelter Cove restaurant say her people had come over as slaves to Daufuskie Island and that Hannay lived there now herself. It wasn't conclusive, but he'd

71

get a photo of Hannay and ask Shirley to show it to these women.

Shirley Elgin had been extraordinarily helpful to him—and she was still a handsome woman.

"I can't thank you enough for putting this all together, Shirley. You have put us well ahead in this investigation. I'll send a photo over to you of the woman who might be involved in this—if you can keep these two women from disappearing before then. This crime ring seems to be a couple of steps ahead of us."

"There's no problem with that," Elgin said. "I will have them both put in protective custody. They were frightened beforehand of what might happen to them if they didn't have protection, after I'd done describing the danger they were in, but both begged to be put in witness protection. And if you're really grateful and I've put you ahead of the game, there's something you can do."

So, Evan agreed to have dinner with Shirley Elgin, at her house, which led to him not getting back to Doug's boat until nearly two in the morning after having promised to deliver the photo of Hannay Mongin to Elgin personally rather than "sending it over." Although much the same age as Evan—and Charlotte—Shirley had aged very well and, always athletic, had kept herself in trim. She was as attractive—and attracting—to Evan as she'd always been. He'd been mooning about Charlotte too long, he thought. What Charlotte and Brenda had was the real deal and he'd just have to accept that.

Evan was whistling happily and had a silly grin on his face when he climbed into Doug's boat. All Doug said was, "So, where's mine?" When Evan just grinned at him, Doug snorted and started preparing the boat for a nighttime cruise back to Hilton Head. He didn't mention that Evan was wearing his shirt inside out. He'd let Evan discover that eventually himself.

* * * *

Hannay Mongin and Otta Stephens caught a ferry at the Broad Creek Marina on Hilton Head for the trip across the Calibogue Sound to the Daufuskie Marina on the Cooper River.

72

They stood at the rail, Hannay's arm around Otta. It had been quite a night. Hannay had been insatiable—just as Otta's friend, Rachel, had said she'd be—and Otta had given the other woman all she wanted. Hannay's free hand was gripping the rail. She was wearing the ivory bracelet she'd had on the night she'd eaten at Bistro 17 in Shelter Cove with Brenda Brandon's crew and Aaron Woolridge. She was purposely wearing it now—to draw Otta out. She knew there had been more than a casual hookup with Otta and the ivory bracelet that had come down through Hannay's family had something to do with that.

"You keep looking at my bracelet," she said. "Have you seen something like this before? I always thought it was a unique family heirloom." Hannay knew Otta had seen something like the bracelet before. Hannay had found a sketch of the bracelet in Otta's purse.

Otta didn't answer; she opened her purse and took the sketch out. "This looks like the same bracelet to me," she said.

"This is why we met, isn't it?" Hannay asked. She took a stronger grip on the other young woman. No one was looking. She knew Otta was a newspaper reporter. If this was about the sex slave business, she could easily heave the young woman over the rail. It would be regrettable because she was attracted to Otta was so good in bed, but if the young woman was nosing around Hannay's side business . . .

"Yes, I came looking for you, I admit it. This bracelet. We both know Rachel. Rachel Moore, in Savannah." Rachel Moore managed a burlesque house. She was a performer who had once been Hannay's lover. Since then, she'd been Otta's lover too.

"Yes, I know Rachel," Hannay said. She still wasn't happy about what this might be about, as Rachel had taken some of the illegal sex workers Hannay had brought into the country. She hadn't asked questions about them, though. As far as Hannay knew, Rachel didn't know the extent of the business Hannay was in. She had every reason to just believe that Hannay had been helping young women in trouble with nowhere else to turn.

"A sketch like this came down through my family," Otta said, "with the legend that the bracelet had been the only link to

Sierra Leone of the woman who was first brought here. She somehow lost the bracelet but did a sketch of it. The sketch, much older and more yellowed than this, is framed and on my living room wall. Rachel saw it and said she'd seen the identical bracelet on your wrist. So, I came looking for you."

Hannay eased her grip. "This bracelet came down through my family here on Daufuskie Island. You said you had a genealogy of your family in the computer? I have hardcopy records of mine. The first order of business, I think, when we get to my cottage, is to compare our records, to see if the families merge at some point."

Hannay was satisfied that the appearance of Otta had nothing to do with present-day sex slaving. She had her own golf cart waiting at the marina landing—everyone on Daufuskie traveled by golf cart. It didn't take long after they'd gotten to Hannay's small, nearly two-hundred-and-fifty-year-old cottage, made of tabby and now painted a startling blue, to see where their family trees intersected.

"Cuffee. His name was Cuffee," Hannay said. "His wife's name was Mercy. Back in the late seventeen hundreds. We both have a Cuffee Mongin, Mongin being the name of the family who owned the plantation here in the Oak Ridge area then, as an ancestor. I'd say we both had him as a granddaddy many times removed. That would be a fascinating tale of how that happened and then the families diverged. Now isn't that something?"

"I'm relieved," Otta said. "It was always a nagging family mystery of what the sketch might mean. This may be as close as I'll ever get to an explanation of that. But it's close enough."

"Would you like to have the bracelet?"

"You should keep it. It's as much a part of your family history as it might be of mine. And your family has given it respectful treatment."

"We should celebrate. I know how I'd like to celebrate," Hannay said.

Otta laughed. "You never get enough, do you?"

"No, I don't. I'm high maintenance and greedy."

"Does it matter now, though, that we're probably related?"

"If you go far enough back, everyone is related to everyone else. It doesn't matter to me if it doesn't matter to you."

It didn't matter to Otta.

Otta woke in midafternoon, overheated and feeling a bit smothered by Hannay, who was sleeping. She managed to extract herself from the other woman's embrace without waking her and she went out to the front porch of the small house, which overlooked a short beach down to the Atlantic Ocean. That was one mystery solved—or at least satisfied with a plausible explanation, although Hannay was right, it would be good to know the whole story of how their families intersected and how a bracelet Otta's ancestor obviously venerated enough to sketch wound up on Hannay's wrist.

That, however, was not the only mystery she was working on, and it wasn't the one paying her bills. The FBI operation she had overheard in planning concerned this island and the mystery of air flights coming and going without any apparent place to land. She turned and looked into the house, which was essentially one room. Hannay was still sleeping on the bed.

Otta returned to the cottage and found her clothes and shoes, which had been unceremoniously dropped in a heap beside the bed. She put them on, without waking Hannay, and left the house to walk into the interior of the island and to do some exploring of her own.

Sometime later Hannay woke to the sound of her cellphone buzzing. Her boss wanted her to take a quick trip to Argentina that night. She, of course, said she would. She didn't really have any say in the matter. It was only then that she remembered that Otta was there with her, staying a "few days" without any definite end. Hannay didn't want the stay to end. But remembering Otta and wondering what to do with her while she was away on business, Hannay realized the young woman wasn't in the house. Maybe she could just stay here alone tonight, Hannay thought.

But where was she? She wasn't anywhere around. She was a reporter. Hannay had to remember that. There was always a danger of what she might be up to. Hannay got into her golf cart and started driving around. She drove straight for the walled Haig Point Club, and that extra fairway. Anyplace else Otta went would be fine. That was where Hannay had to be sure Otta wasn't nosing around.

When she got to the wall closing off the fairway, she saw what she was hoping not to see. Otta was at the wall. It was unclear whether she had stayed on this side or was climbing down from being on the other side of the wall. If she'd been on the other side, she was close enough to see the airplane under the camouflage netting.

Hannay put on a smile and tooted the horn of the golf cart. Otta saw her and walked to the cart.

"I was just taking a walk," Otta said as she got into the cart.

Hannay gave her a close look, but Otta seemed not to be hiding anything. Of course, newspaper reporters would be trained to do that. "Daufuskie may be the safest place on earth to do that," she said. "It's so isolated and there's nothing really to see here." If the woman had seen an airplane under camouflage netting, surely she'd say something. At least she would if she didn't suspect Hannay of being involved in whatever that was.

Hannay's mind was racing, but she continued to act as if nothing was amiss. "Let's go home and get something to eat."

The something to eat that Hannay provided included a knockout drug for Otta. She was a larger woman than Otta was, so she had no trouble getting Otta into the cart and driving her a short distance away to the other small cottage Hannay had inherited. It was known as Cuffee's Cottage and always had been as far as she knew. Until today, she'd had no idea of what the significance was of the name "Cuffee."

Before she flew out with Craig Little and Butch that night, she called Pegg, the bartender owner at Pegg's over on Hilton Head, and asked her friend to place an anonymous phone call for her. It was the best she could do on the spur of the moment, although she knew she should have done something more terminal.

* * * *

Speaking of high-maintenance women, DeeDee Yance had been pouting for two days, all alone in Trent Nichols's ostentatious walled mansion compound on the beach at the Haig Point Club gated golf club community on Daufuskie Island. Trent had been holed up in his studio with his band and hangers on, none of whom paid much attention to DeeDee, preparing for a coming concert. DeeDee was from an entirely different world from Trent—and certainly from most of his friends. And the bodyguards the man kept around him—and watching her—intimidated her no end.

The island wasn't her idea of living the high life. She was a Hollywood girl, all razzle and dazzle. Daufuskie Island was so laid back it might has well be asleep. And Trent Nichols basically was a good-old-boy redneck—or, more to the point, a bad-boy redneck. This Sunday afternoon wasn't the first time she had wondered why she'd married the man. She had become resolved to it having been a snap decision on the rebound. She couldn't have the suave actor Tony Trice, so she'd gone for his complete opposite.

She was going stir crazy in the mansion. She had to get out. She'd been in the pool and she'd been down to the beach and the private pier, which were reached by a steep wooden staircase from the back swimming pool terrace. She hadn't been anywhere else on the island. The mansion compound backed onto the Haig Point golf links, but she'd never been in that direction. In the mansion, she felt like the whole staff was watching her, ready to report anything unusual to Trent. He had turned out to be more controlling than she could possibly have imagined him to be. What could he have to hide on this sleepy island?

She had to get out of the house. She decided to walk out on the golf course. She didn't want to walk around the streets lined with other mansions of the famous but reclusive. She didn't want to talk to anyone. She wanted to be recognized, yes. She was a vain movie actress. She wanted people to recognize her, but she didn't want to talk to any of them. They'd had all been celebrities for something too, and she'd feel dumb for not knowing who they were or knowing that they were as famous, or more so, than she was. So, she walked into the woods across from the front of the house, toward a golf fairway, and into the interior of Daufuskie Island.

She almost ran into one of Trent's bodyguards, the one who disturbed her the most, one who always looked at her with dead eyes, both as if he would take her if he could and as if she was just Trent's "piece," just a piece of property. She faded into the foliage just in time as the bodyguard, Butch, passed her, walking deliberately to the back corner of the Nichols compound, where she could see an outbuilding.

When Butch was gone, she continued on, over to a fairway, and she walked around the edge of that, knowing enough about golf that those who weren't playing the course should stay off the course and at the same time be on the lookout for golf balls in the air. Strangely enough, though, she didn't see anyone playing this fairway. That was strange, as it was a Sunday, and she'd heard that the course was in great demand on the weekends.

She quickly learned there was something out here more strange than the fairway not being used. When she saw the funny-looking airplane under the camouflage netting, she couldn't process that being there for the longest several minutes.

What the hell? Trent needed to know about this. This was just beyond their back property line. She turned to head back to the house and almost fell over the man's body. He was lying in a pool of blood and there was a bullet hole in his back. He clearly was dead. She let out a piercing scream and took off, blindly stumbling through the foliage, not bothering to look for a path. In thrashing about in the underbrush, she came close to the outbuilding in the corner of the Nichols compound. The bodyguard, Butch, who had gone in the direction when she was headed to the fairway, came running out of the building, having heard her scream.

"There's a dead man . . . and an airplane . . . back there," she managed to scream at him, nonsensically, as she ran past.

Butch followed her. As she raced around the house, headed toward Trent's music studio, she could see their cabin cruiser pulling away from the pier. Trent and his buddies were in it.

DeeDee cried out to her husband as she got to the top of the wooden staircase down to the beach and the pier, but he either didn't hear her or didn't care. Halfway down the staircase, she stopped, realizing that the boat wasn't going to stop steaming out toward the Atlantic. She turned, her next thought being to get back to the house and call 911.

The only problem with that was that the bodyguard, Butch, was now standing at the top of the wooden stairs.

Chapter Seven: Shutting Down

Monday, 6 May 2019

Both Brenda and Charlotte were humming and touching each other affectionately in passing as they worked in the kitchen in the morning on breakfast. Neither could help smiling to each other and to themselves, and, although it was partly from relief and happiness that Marilyn was well and beyond a cancer scare, it wasn't only that. Evan Worthington and Douglas Dolan joined them for breakfast in the Shelter Cove condo, and Evan too was humming and smiling. Doug was smiling as well, but his was more of a knowing and amused smile. When Tony and Michelle arrived from their own condo at the other side of the building, to join them, their smiles and hums joined the medley. All but Doug Dolan had had a humdinger of a night, and he, at least, had gotten some amusement out of the night's events.

Over breakfast they sobered up a bit, and when Tony and Michelle left, Tony back to the condo to study his movie script and Michelle to the golf course to practice her golf, the rest settled down to their battle plans.

"Doug will take us all over to Daufuskie in his boat," Even said. "He'll first take me around to the Cooper River landing, where the Burches will meet me and we'll start our search, starting with the extra Haig Point Club fairway Charlotte found on the aerial shots yesterday. Then he'll take you around the island to Nichols's private pier. It looks like the fairway I'll be looking for abuts the Nichols property at the back. Charlotte, when you are able, you could take a look at what's what from that side."

"Will do," Charlotte said. "Brenda is the one Nichols really wants there. I assume I'll be free to do as I please as long as I stay out of his way."

"Damn," Evan said as Doug's boat made its approach to the Cooper River landing.

"What's the matter?" Charlotte asked, coming up beside Evan at the boat railing.

"There's a police launch at the pier, with its lights going. I didn't want this to be a high-profile police operation. I see some uniforms and Margaret and David are on the pier. At least they could turn the damn police lights off. I hope this isn't Shirley's doing. She's been very helpful but maybe a bit too zealous to help?"

"Shirley?" Charlotte asked, surprised.

"Yes. Shirley Elgin. She's agent in charge in Savannah now. She's the one who took me to the brothels yesterday to interview the women who had been brought into the country to work as illegals."

"Ah, yes, the brothel you were at when we spoke on the phone. Shirley's in Savannah now? She was in Charleston."

"Yes, she was. She's moved. Are you displeased she's giving us help on this?"

"Of course not. We need all the help we can get."

Worthington seemed almost disappointed that there was no resentment or even a hint of jealousy there. But then, they had been docked and he was getting off the boat and heading toward the Burches to find out what was up with the policemen on the scene.

Charlotte, Brenda, and Doug encountered more of the same when they came around the island and approached the private Nichols dock. Two police boats, lights flashing, were already there, and police were swarming around the beach and up on the house's terrace like it was a crime scene.

And that's what it turned out to be—a crime scene.

Doug pulled his sleek cabin cruiser in on the other side of the pier from Trent Nichols's larger and sleeker cabin cruiser. A policeman on the pier tried to wave them off, but Charlotte had her FBI ID out and said they had been invited to be house guests of Trent Nichols. The policeman recognized Brenda, became tongue tied, and let them pass. Charlotte didn't bother to ask him what the problem was. She saw who obviously was the officer in charge and made a beeline for him up the beach with her ID held in front of her.

The policeman practically saluted her and answered her question straightway. "There's been an accident here," he said. "The guy who owns this place is a rock star."

"Yes, I know. Trent Nichols. He and his wife invited my friend and me to spend a couple of days here. He's married to a friend of ours, the movie actress, DeeDee Yance. What's the problem?"

"You knew DeeDee Yance?" the policeman asked.

The past tense didn't escape Charlotte's notice. "Is that who's had the accident?"

"Yes, she apparently tumbled down these stairs and down to the beach. Broke her neck. One of their security men found her. The husband was out fishing with friends and was called back to the house before they called us."

"My friend back there is Brenda Brandon, the movie actress," Charlotte said. "She worked with DeeDee. Maybe I'd better—"

"I hate to ask you, but the husband won't take a look at the body. Could either you or Miss Brandon—?"

"I'll do it. No problem. Lead on," Charlotte said. "Just a moment, though, please. Is it OK if I send Miss Brandon back to Hilton Head? She wasn't here earlier today. She's never been on the island before. I can vouch for that. There's no need for her to get tied up in this." Charlotte didn't fully know why, but, for some reason, she thought she needed to get Brenda away from here and somewhere safe pronto.

"Certainly," the policeman said.

Charlotte went back and told Brenda and Doug what happened. "I think it's best that you take Brenda back to Shelter Cove, Doug, and then bring the boat back here."

"Maybe I should stay," Brenda said.

"Maybe you shouldn't," Charlotte said, giving her a meaningful look. "I'm going to have work to do here, I think. And I'll do it best if I didn't have to worry about your safety."

"I'm worried about your safety, Charlotte."

"That's great to know, love, but could you go back with Doug now and let me get on with it here? This is what I do, Brenda."

"Of course," Brenda said, giving right in. "Phone me as soon as you can, though."

"Of course."

"I'll worry about you every moment."

"Which I'll love you for. Now go." She had turned and said that to Doug.

"Aye, aye, Cap," Doug said and went back to untying the ropes he had tied.

"Terrible. An accident, you say?" Brenda asked as she stepped back into the boat.

"That's what someone is saying, but I'm not sold on coincidences," Charlotte responded. "I *will* phone you later. I promise. And thanks for worrying." She turned her bulk to the wooden stairs up to the terrace of the Nichols house, already seeing the steep staircase as an enemy.

* * * *

Otta Stephens woke slowly and groggily from her drugged state. She was on a bed, so her first thought was being with Hannay on her Daufuskie Island cottage bed. There was much the same sense of Hannay's cottage where she now was— the tabby walls and the small size of it—but increasingly as she came back into the world, Otta realized she wasn't in Hannay's Daufuskie cottage. It was similar but not the same. It was more primitive. There was less furniture, and what there was was cruder, more basically functional. The bed was a rope bed, the mattress thin. She was dressed in her T-shirt and jeans. When she last was aware, she was just in her panties, sitting at Hannay's table, eating dinner with her.

Panic didn't start to set in until Otta realized she had an iron ankle restraint on her leg attached to a rusted chain that, in turn, was attached to the wall next to the bed. The chain was long, but when she rolled off the bed and moved toward the door to the hut, she realized she couldn't reach that far. She also couldn't reach the old and scarred dresser by the door, where she could see a key was located. She could only hope that it was the key to the leg irons on her ankle.

She wasn't in immediate danger. There was a bowl of biscuits and a jug of water near enough to the bed for her to reach and a form of porta john—a low cabinet with a porcelain bowl in it and even a roll of toilet paper. She could exist here for a short while, at least. That gave her hope that she wasn't meant to be left here to die. But she couldn't last for long.

Why had this happened? What had she done or not done? Where had she made Hannay suspicious enough of her to do this to her? There couldn't be anyone else who was responsible for this. This had to be Hannay. But why? And to what end? If she had angered Hannay enough to do this to her, why hadn't she angered the woman enough to kill her—at least yet?

She'd almost been able to calm down enough to start calculating options when she heard the sound of movement outside the hut. She knew she was near the ocean, because she could hear the sound of the surf. She couldn't see out because, although she could reach the two windows on the opposite sides of the small building, they were shuttered and padlocked. The place smelled musty and stale. She didn't think anyone lived here—not for a very long time. She didn't think that anyone could do so. Hannay had kept her cottage up. Although it was small, it was quite livable. This one was like Hannay's cottage must have been nearly two-hundred-and-fifty years ago when Hannay said her ancestors lived here as slaves.

Was the movement Hannay returning? Was it someone she wanted to know she was here or someone she didn't? If it was Hannay, she'd come inside eventually on her own.

"Hello? Anyone here? Anyone inside?" The voice was male—not Hannay.

Otta was torn between calling out and curling up on the bed, trying to disappear into the musty tabby wall.

"Hello. Bluffton police here. Anyone inside? We were told there was someone here who needed assistance."

Otta started screaming hysterically. "Here. I'm here. I'm chained to the wall. Help me!"

"How did you know I was here and chained?" she asked once the policemen forced their way inside and released her.

"We received a telephone call, with directions on where you could be found. We came as soon as we got the call. Who are you? And what were you doing on Daufuskie?"

Hannay, Otta thought. She didn't let me die. She told someone where to find me in time. What should I say? How much should I tell them about her? Should I tell them to go to her house—that she might be there? Should I see that she's arrested?

"I'm a reporter with the *Savannah Morning News*," she said. "There is evidence of a sex slave ring operating from this island and I was just investigating it." There, she'd keep Hannay out of this for now, at least. It would give her time to talk with Hannay on why she did this. Otta was so confused by all of this, and it wasn't just effect of the drugs she'd been given.

"You weren't . . . men didn't . . . ?" The policeman was trying to find a way to ask her if she'd been assaulted. She'd said she was investigating a possible sex slave ring.

"Oh, my no," she said, as she got into one of two golf carts the four policemen had arrived in. "I haven't been hurt."

"We'll take you back to the Cooper River landing. Our lieutenant is there—and a man from the FBI has arrived. If this is about sex trafficking . . ."

A man from the FBI? she thought. So, the belief that there's sex trafficking operating from this island is true and being played out as were the plans she'd overheard. Could she get a scoop? She had almost forgotten about Hannay Mongin, but then she had reason to remember her. As she got into the golf cart, she felt something in the pocket of her jeans. She pulled out the ivory bracelet that had started her search for Hannay in the first place. She turned to look back at the cottage as they were rumbling away and almost exclaimed. A wood plaque with lettering burned into it declared "Cuffee's Cabin."

When they were driving up to the pier at the Cooper River landing, she recognized the tall, distinguished-looking man who had been in charge of the sex trafficking search meeting she'd overheard and recorded at the Mediterranean Harbour

Grill at Shelter Cover. As she approached, she could see that he recognized her too.

He flashed his ID. "Evan Worthington of the FBI. Didn't I see you a couple of nights ago at the Bistro 17 restaurant in Shelter Cover over on Hilton Head?"

"Yes," she answered, flashing her *Savannah Morning News* credentials.

"You want to tell me what this is all about, young lady?"

OK, this was the time to be as straight with him as her brief allowed, Otta thought, if she had any chance of getting a scoop on the FBI operation that obviously was under way here. There was, of course, lying and then there was just omission. She wouldn't tell them any more about Hannay than she could avoid telling them.

* * * *

They had left DeeDee's body where it had landed, three-quarters of the way down the wooden staircase, her head propped at an angle against the banister, where her neck had broken. She wasn't dressed for the beach. Charlotte, of course, took note of that when they had lifted the sheet and she'd officially identified the body.

"Is the husband here?" she asked.

"Yes, up on the terrace with the security guard who found the body. In fact, the guard said he'd seen her fall. He said he'd called to her from above and when she'd turned, she'd lost her footing and come down the stairs."

"Did he say if he knew why she was coming down to the shore? She isn't dressed for the beach."

"You noticed that, did you?" the policeman said, impressed with how quick the older, intimidatingly large woman was on the uptake. He'd seen the FBI credentials, but she wasn't anything like he expected of an FBI agent. She was old, and although nice enough looking, she was a large woman, and didn't move agilely. She was rather awkward and walked off center. He wondered if perhaps she'd been wounded earlier in her career. Still, she was obviously quite sharp. When she looked around her, he got the impression that the woman took in everything.

Trent Nichols was sitting in a patio chair by the pool when Charlotte had huffed up the stairs to him. The policeman had followed along behind her, prepared to keep her from falling back while knowing that, if she did, with her bulk she'd carry them both down to the same fate DeeDee Yance had suffered. It was his duty to protect, though, and he did it resolutely if with trepidation.

"Trent? Remember me? Brenda Brandon's friend? You invited us here today."

"Yes, I remember," he said. He was having trouble focusing on her, though. Was it drugs or alcohol? He'd been spacey the other night too. He was a rock star, so she guessed both and she guessed that it was his usual state, that it didn't have much if anything to do with his wife, finally being removed from the stairs below now that she'd been official identified.

She showed him her FBI consultant ID, upon which he'd done a double take and acquired a hunted look. Maybe DeeDee had neglected to tell her husband that Brenda's spouse was a fed.

Nichols immediately went off into a mumbled rant about himself and how all of this was putting him out. Charlotte didn't discern a mention of DeeDee in the ramble. She wasn't surprised about this either.

"And this is the man who saw her fall down the stairs," the policeman gestured to a solidly built bodyguard-type male in his late twenties or early thirties standing behind where Nichols was sitting. Doing his security guard job to the hilt, Charlotte surmised. He was a good-looking man, if hard looking. A marine type but one who had seen and engaged in hard duty. "Benjamin Schmidt," The policeman said.

"People call me Butch," the man said, his voice laced with suspicion and hard attitude. Charlotte was showing him her FBI credentials. His eyes narrowed and became cold as ice. Charlotte marked him immediately as someone to watch. The policeman asked Butch to relate his story again, and he did so, almost word for word identical with what the policeman had quoted from him when he and Charlotte were on the staircase with DeeDee's body. The explanation sounded rehearsed.

This is nothing new for him, Charlotte assessed. He's got this down pat. He'd seen death before. Might even have been involved in creating it.

Whatever it was to Trent Nichols, it was all about him. He went off into a rant again, distracting Charlotte and policeman. When she looked up again, Butch, the security guy, was striding away, around the side of the house.

"Excuse me," Charlotte said, and, on instinct, she followed Butch.

He led her to the back corner of the property on narrow paths bordered by dense foliage. Charlotte did what she could to keep him from knowing she was there. Luckily, he was in white tennis gear and easy to spot through the underbrush and she was in green, easy to hide.

She followed him to a small outbuilding at the corner of the property well camouflaged by the foliage. He went in but didn't stay long. Charlotte moved off to behind some trees when he came out. He passed her, going off in another direction, not back toward the house. Charlotte crept up to a window in the back of the building and looked in, doing a double take from what she saw.

There were three young women, on beds, with ankle irons chaining them to the walls next to their beds. They were all lying on the beds, their eyes shut. Charlotte could tell they were breathing, but, when she rapped on the window, they didn't respond. That's what Butch had been doing in the building, Charlotte surmised—drugging the women to keep them quiet while the police were crawling over the property. They were all young and beautiful. One was black and the other two dark, probably all Hispanics. Charlotte wondered if this was where Maria Silva had started what was left of her life as an illegal alien from Brazil, brought to the States by someone else—someone engaged in the international sex trade.

She was about to go around to the front of the building to enter, try to revive the young women, and release them if she could, when she heard a gunshot and cries from beyond the property line, out by one of the golf club fairways. One of the voices was Evan's. Another one was David Burch's. So, she headed for the voices, meeting up with Evan on the edge of the fairway where camouflage netting had been extended over the trees. The tire marks told her that they had found where the airplane that was transporting these women from South America was kept.

The body of a dead man nearby told her that Steve McCall, the novelist, had somehow gotten himself killed before they could get to the island to follow up on the leads he'd given them. She knew a dead man who had been dead for some time from one who would have been killed by the gunshot she just heard. This man had bled out and the blood wasn't fresh. She had no more a few seconds to experience the regret of helpful citizens who get in the way of the bad guys being pursued by the good guys, but she took the moment to mentally thank McCall for his help and to resolve to ensure that his effort hadn't been in vain.

She didn't have more time than that to hook up with Evan, David, and Margaret, though, before they were racing back toward the Nichols house.

"Yes, I saw him," Evan called out to Charlotte as he answered her "I'm over here" cry. "A tragedy. These guys are in it for keeps. A goon took a shot at us when he'd seen we'd found where the plane was kept."

"They're keeping the women over this way in a building. They've been drugged. They look comfortable enough but they are chained to the wall. The man who shot at you must be Butch, Trent Nichols's bodyguard. DeeDee Yance has been killed over by the house. I wouldn't be surprised if Butch—"

"OK, let's go after him," Evan called out, and they all ran to and around the house—to be in time to see Trent's cabin cruiser steaming away from the pier, with Trent and Butch in the bridge. A surprised contingent of policemen stood by, immobile, watching, no doubt surprised at how fast the rock star could move when under threat.

Doug Dolan was coming into the pier from another direction. Flashing his credentials, Evan grabbed a couple of the policemen and, with Charlotte, David, and Margaret, arrived at the pier to meet Dolan's boat. They all climbed on board and took out after Nichols's cruiser. He was too far ahead of them, though, and was in international waters before the authorities could reach him.

* * * *

"You summoned us, saying it was an emergency. We had to come away without our copilot. I hope the risk was worth it."

"I believe it is, Ms. Mongin."

"I would not have come on such short notice if you weren't one of our best suppliers, Julio," she said. Hannay Mongin was in the office of an exclusive strip club and brothel in Buenos Aires, Argentina. Her pilot, Craig Little, was standing behind her, looking through a one-way glass window at the club's performance stage, where quite a performance was going on. His tongue was nearly hanging out.

"I think you will thank me. Esmeralda is one of our best girls, and she will go with you willingly—happily. Gratefully."

"I will determine if she goes with us," Hannay said, still clearly irritated that she was called away from Daufuskie Island on such short notice. She had had to make a decision on Otta Stephens, and she hadn't made a clear one in one direction or the other. With the suspicion she had of what the reporter was up to, she should have informed her boss and he would have taken care of the woman. But, having found a family connection with Otta, not to mention a highly satisfying sexual connection as well, she hadn't made the fully protective decision. She'd arranged for Otta to be freed. Now what? For the first time in her life, perhaps, Hannay had not thought a problem all the way through and taken decisive action to protect herself. What now?

"Why is the woman so willing to go with us? Why are you willing to give her up if she's so good for business?"

"Esmeralda saw something a client had done that she shouldn't see. She was a favorite of his. He's given me a day to get her out of Argentina forever and someplace the Argentine authorities can't get to her—won't even have any idea what she knows; what she's seen. I'm just trying to solve her problem and give you a good deal as well."

"You know I won't take her on speculation—even from you, Julio. You know that she must be tried out first."

90

"I have told her that she must please you before you will take her."

"And my male associate here, as well. I want her to do her job with both men and women."

"Of course," Julio said, standing. "Which of you first? Follow me, and I will take you to her."

"I always come first," Hannay said, with a slight smirk on her lovely lips.

Later, as Craig Little was off doing his sampling, and a smiling and much happier Hannay had returned to Julio's office to share in champagne and more detailed arrangements for the return trip, with Esmeralda included, to the States, Hannay expressed her complete satisfaction with Esmeralda's talents and willingness.

She and Julio had just finished with a toast when he looked over her shoulder, through the two-way glass. His eyes bugged out, and he exclaimed, "Holy hell!"

"What?" Hannay asked. But he didn't answer. He merely gestured beyond her. Hannay turned and looked through the glass out onto the club's performance floor to see countless Argentine policemen pouring into the room, their eyes focused on the office Julio and Hannay were in, moving like a flood in their direction.

* * * *

Giving up the chase of Trent Nichols's cabin cruiser, Evan Worthington and his FBI operation colleagues returned to Daufuskie Island and started into the laborious work of taking stock and bringing the Bluffton police force into the picture.

The three women they released from the building at the back of the Nichols property were a great help once they had been brought out from under the influence of the drugs that had been given them to keep them quiet and translators had been brought in.

The buck didn't stop with the security guard, Butch, as far as kidnapping the women and bringing them into the country illegally to serve eventually as sex slaves up and down the East Coast of the States. Hannay Mongin's role in acquiring and transporting them, as well as that of Craig Little, was established. Evan thought it went higher than that—it was a very expensive operation—and he was right. The women weren't being saved for brothels. They had been required to service men here on Daufuskie Island, starting with Trent Nichols himself. From what the women said, Trent was treated by Butch and Hannay and all of Trent's band friends who were in on the opportunity, as the boss. That, coupled with how quickly Trent Nichols had absconded, was good enough evidence of Nichols's guilt for Evan, at least for now. He called in an arrest call for Trent Nichols and Benjamin Schmidt, also known as Butch.

He would have put in a call for Hannay Mongin's arrest too, if Shirley Elgin hadn't beaten him to it. While he was debriefing the three women, Shirley called to report that she'd gotten a photo and background information on Hannay Mongin herself—the woman's photo was all over the Charleston Film Festival Web site—and had spent the night tracking the woman's criminal background down and her connections with sex slavers in South America. She had found that Hannay had flown into Buenos Aires in the night. The FBI agent had then coordinated with the Argentine police to have Mongin and Little seized and arrested.

"Thanks, Shirley," a stunned Evan had said on the phone. "I owe you way more than a dinner for this." He heard Charlotte snort as he clicked off.

"Shirley knows you owe her much more. And you can bet she knows just how to collect."

Evan gave Charlotte an embarrassed look—but he didn't bother to disagree with her. In fact, he looked quite pleased, which wasn't lost on Charlotte.

Otta Stephens and her incarceration hadn't been overlooked, but no one quite knew how she fit into the equation. She wasn't claiming to even know Hannay Mongin, let alone Trent Nichols or the security guard, Butch. And she was a reporter for a Savannah newspaper. Everyone was tiptoeing around her, not wanting to be part of a newspaper story she may be writing. She did reveal to Evan enough about what she knew of the sex slaving that he promised, after checking up the line, to give her first release of information on having broken the ring up.

In the end, they decided to believe that she'd been kidnapped by persons unidentified and unknown to her to be included in the sex slave captures. It wasn't an elegant solution, but it was the best they could do.

Charlotte's eyes narrowed when she saw the ivory bracelet on Otta's wrist. Always observant, Charlotte remembered having seen it on Hannay's wrist the other day. Charlotte couldn't assess what that was all about, but she decided to keep an eagle eye on Otta as the rest of the case unwound. Perhaps she'd have a private talk with the young woman later.

Chapter Eight: Getting Back to the Rest of It

Ten Days Later

Returning from a memorial service for the novelist, Steve McCall, whose ashes were being taken out into the ocean from Harbour Town at the southern tip of Hilton Head Island, Charlotte Diamond and Brenda Boynton were meeting with Charlotte's brother and sister-in-law, Chance and Marilyn Diamond, at the Shelter Cove condo for lunch. Marilyn had been buoyant now that her cancer scare was over and, although he had aged considerably in appearance, Chance had been greatly relieved and was solicitous of Marilyn's every mood and move.

"Hi ho, other Diamonds," Charlotte called out as she and Brenda entered the condo.

"Hi ho, yourself," Marilyn called back. "You're just in time for lunch. Shall we eat out on the balcony and watch the activity in the marina?"

"Of course," Charlotte answered. "We might as well enjoy what we're paying high prices for. Have you two managed without us? Were you going house hunting in Wexford Plantation today? I haven't heard much about this since you two came back from Charleston."

"Oh, we've decided not to leave Williamsburg," Marilyn answered as she fussed with getting the balcony table set. "We thought about it. Through Chance's medical practice and my work with the Williamsburg area churches, we figure that we have established quite a network of good will supporters. We might as well stay in Williamsburg and enjoy that support net."

"Oh 'we' have, have we?" Charlotte said, with a chuckle and a meaningful look at Chance, who grinned back at her and winked.

If Marilyn caught the inference and import of that in her change of attitude about sleeping with the ancestors by relocating to the former Baldwin plantation area, she made no indication she had. The others were happy to just let that go. The old Marilyn was back and everyone else was relieved and grateful for that.

"So, is Mr. McCall floating on the waves now?" she asked as they sat down to lunch. Marilyn didn't ask that flippantly. She realized what the man had sacrificed to do the right thing.

"Yes, I assume so," Brenda answered. "We didn't take the boat out. There were few mourners, I'm afraid. Mostly from his publishing house. Sad, really. He had no one close apparently."

"He probably was alone from living on that isolated island for so long," Charlotte remarked. "His publisher said that they found an almost completed novel in his house, which they will, with Steve's mother's permission and to her benefit, finish off with a ghostwriter and publish. It's a parallel mystery to the real one he lost his life helping us combat, so there is a bittersweet angle to getting that novel published. He'll live on in that, at least."

"Speaking of mothers, is that dreadful Helen Jones still storming around and making demands?" Chance asked. He was looking at Brenda, who had received most of the attention from Helen Jones, who was DeeDee Yance's stage mother parent and who had been the bane of ever movie production Brenda had been in with DeeDee.

"Yes," Brenda answered. "We all assumed she'd be taking DeeDee back to St. Louis, where DeeDee's family is from and Helen lives, for burial there, but Helen wants the full funeral performance out at Forest Lawn near Hollywood. She wants me to be there and she wants all of the publicity she can get for the burial and for DeeDee's tragic life. I'll do what I can, of course, but then I hope there isn't another daughter in the wings for Helen to helicopter."

"You've already done a lot," Marilyn said. Brenda had gone ahead with the two film festival events, the one in Charleston, having now been hosted by Aaron Woolridge in the absence of the arrested Hannay Mongin, and the one in Savannah. Brenda had wrapped the theme of the events around DeeDee, who had appeared in one of the feature films, *White Orchid Found*. As well as giving a tribute to the young actress that she deserved, beyond her mother pushing for it, this relieved Brenda from having to talk about more personal and painful connections to the films being shown in scene excerpts. The first film screened, *Woman Scorned*, had been used as a template for a murder she was implicated in and the second, *White Orchid Found*, was related to revealing that one of the stars—and DeeDee's boyfriend at the time, Tony Trice—was Brenda's love child.

In the intervening week, the charity golf tournament had played out, with Tony Trice filling in for the escaped rock star, Trent Nichols, and Doug Dolan, to the surprise of all his friends having been revealed as a national pro-Am golf contender, for the deceased Steve McCall. Brenda and Michelle Minor's foursome had the most fans following them, although neither of them won any prizes with the golf, Michelle being distracted by something else and Brenda not being much of a golfer.

"I wonder if those taking McCall's ashes out to sea encountered Trent Nichols still floating in circles in international waters," Chance said. "I wonder if he knows there are reports of a hurricane brewing out there."

"Of course there are reports of a hurricane and there have been deaths on this vacation," Charlotte said, with a laugh. "We have you along. There always is catastrophic weather and deaths when we vacation with you, Chance." Everyone laughed, as that, indeed was the book on going on vacation with Chance Diamond.

"I always thought it was you who was the curse," Chance gamely responded. "You seem to collect dead bodies even when I'm not around."

Afraid Chance was making too much sense with that rejoinder, Charlotte continued. "But don't worry about Trent Nichols. He's undoubtedly off doing the concert tour rounds in countries without extradition agreements with the United States, and his faithful bodyguard, Butch, is likely sticking close to his side for his own good. We'll get them both eventually, though."

"I've been reading the report on the closedown of the sex slave trafficking ring in the *Savannah Morning News*, Charlotte," Chance said. "Good coverage of you and Evan—and of that woman FBI agent in Savannah, Shirley Elgin, but I was surprised that the byline wasn't of that young woman reporter who was almost caught up in it on the island."

"Otta Stephens?" Charlotte asked. "Yes, it was strange that she gave up the opportunity to get the scoop on the reporting. Evan had promised her she'd get the first crack at the story and then she turned it down when she could have done the reporting."

"Where's Evan?" Marilyn asked, turning to Charlotte. "I thought he was coming back with you to have lunch with us."

"He met up with Shirley Elgin at Steve McCall's memorial service," Brenda interjected. "And the two of them went to lunch together."

Both Chance and Marilyn looked away and dropped the issue, being unsure of what Charlotte's reaction to Evan going off with the Elgin woman was. If they'd looked at her, though, they would have seen she was smiling, happy that Evan might have found someone to settle down with at last who was someone who was willing and able to do that with him.

"And Doug Dolan?" Marilyn asked, looking at Brenda this time.

"He's off on the water again," Brenda answered, without a hint of regret. "He took his cabin cruiser out with those dropping Steve McCall's ashes, and then he was just going to keep on sailing to who knows where? He's a free spirit at heart."

"Speaking of lunch guests, I thought Tony and Michelle would be here for lunch," Charlotte said, preventing any follow up to the Douglas Dolan issue.

"They are busy," Marilyn said, somewhat cryptically and then changed the subject again—or apparently seemed to be changing the subject, although she wasn't, in fact changing it. "You two kept this afternoon at 3:00 p.m. open for our surprise, didn't you?"

"Of course," Charlotte said, looking at Brenda and raising an eyebrow.

The surprise concerned what Tony had stayed behind to talk with Marilyn about the day she came out of surgery. At 3:00 p.m. that afternoon at the end of the island on the Disney Resort island at Hilton Head's Shelter Cover, at the entrance into the yacht basin from Broad Creek, Marilyn stood before Tony Trice and Michelle Minor, Bible in hand, and, with an astonished and tearing Charlotte and Brenda in attendance along with Chance, Evan Worthington, Shirley Elgin, and Aaron Woolridge, she reconfirmed and publicly rededicated Tony and Michelle as man and wife.

Also standing in the background was the *Savannah Morning News* reporter, Otta Stephens, claiming her promised news scoop. The public confirmation of the marriage of the heartthrob movie actor, Tony Trice, son of Brenda Brandon, to the professional tennis player, Michelle Minor, was a much better national news scoop for Otta than the breakup of a sex slave trafficking operation would have been.

* * * *

Later that afternoon, Otta Stephens arrived at the Broad River Correctional Institute in Colombia, South Carolina, where she had already gone twice in recent days. She was visiting Hannay Mongin there. Hannay was being held at the facility as the South Carolina-based case against her was being put together. Otta had found that she couldn't be the one to write up the story of the downfall of a woman who was distantly related to her and who had had a torrid, if brief, relationship with her. More to the point, she couldn't forget that Hannay had spared her life when it was much more to Hannay's benefit to remove her as a threat. She couldn't help Hannay legally, but she could at least let the woman know she wasn't totally alone and fully forgotten. Otta sat for a few minutes in her car, composing herself by fingering the ivory bracelet on her wrist. Then, heaving a sigh of resignation, she climbed out of her car and walked toward the prison's visitors' center.

Epilogue

The glitterati had gathered in the Dolby Theatre in Hollywood for the ninety-second running of the Academy Awards of the Academy of Motion Picture Arts and Sciences. They were down to the awarding of the Oscar for best supporting actress. It wasn't all that much of a surprise when the winner was announced to be Brenda Brandon for her run-away role as the mother of the governor's wife in the film *The Gentleman Pirate*.

The only one in the theater who was truly surprised was the ever-humble Brenda Brandon, who tinkled her signature laugh, smiled her legendary smile, rose from her seat, and, with much of the world watching, leaned down and kissed her partner, Charlotte Diamond, fully on the lips. After giving her spouse a beaming smile and mouthing "I love you," again for all the world to see, Brenda walked up the aisle and onto the stage to thank both her long-time producer, Aaron Woolridge, for giving her yet another fascinating role to work with and her spouse, Charlotte Diamond, without whose support she could not continue to work—and indeed, without her investigative support Brenda probably would not even be free to work and live as she pleased.

As she approached the stage, she passed a beaming Arron Woolridge and his not-so-beaming wife, Cheryl Chandler, who had not received a nomination nod for her leading lady role in *The Gentleman Pirate*.

Afterward Brenda and Charlotte met up with Tony and Michelle and Evan and Shirley Elgin, whose marriage in Annapolis they had just left to attend the Academy Awards, and who were, as the actress's wedding gift, Brenda's guests at the ceremony.

"That's great, Mom," Tony said. "We knew you were a shoo-in for the Oscar."

"Hearing you call me mom is worth more than an Oscar, Tony," she responded. "Next year it will be you." It wasn't just parental pride that was saying that. The script Tony had been working on at Hilton Head the previous spring had turned, after a long delay in filming, into a role in the movie that he was already being acclaimed for.

Evan Worthington then stepped up to the bat. After congratulating Brenda, Evan turned to Charlotte and said, "I think you will be relieved to know that Trent Nichols and Butch Schmidt have been apprehended at last. Nichols apparently didn't know the United States has an extradition treaty with Mauritius and he scheduled a highly publicized concert there."

"That's good to hear," Charlotte responded. "It's good to close out our FBI case at last—perhaps our last one together? I'm getting too old to be chasing suspects."

"Well, about that," Evan said. "I was rather hoping that you and Brenda were up for a little cruise."

"A little cruise?" Charlotte asked. "You want to send us on a cruise?"

"One that involves drugs and arms smuggling and terrorism in the South Seas," Evan said with a straight face. "Just the sort of vacation you two are specialists in. Doesn't that sound appealing?"

Charlotte turned and looked at Brenda, who, raising her "I got another one" Oscar, answered with her signature tinkling laugh and legendary smile.

Bonus Story: Isata's Lament

The late 1770s
The Barrier Islands, South Carolina

Isata was being hauled out of the small, open vessel that had brought her here to this heavily forested land from across the water, where the larger, ocean-going slaver ship had landed at a port town after many days on what she had been told was the Middle Passage from her home in Sierra Leone, Africa, to the New Land. Others had been taken here before, she'd been told, by the English slavers on the island in the mouth of the river not far from her village—where she had been sold by Mingo because she had lain with his sister Otta in preference to laying with him.

A tall, large, muscular man as ebony as she was but dressed like the European sailors who had brought her here in the ship and who had taken her away periodically from the dark cabin where she and a couple of other young women had been held and had covered her, was separating her off from the other captives. He urged her up onto the river bank from the vessel. White men were herding the others in one direction, and the ebony buck was nudging her up onto a dirt road leading into the trees.

She was shackled at the wrists and hobbled at the ankles. The man wasn't pushing her hard, though. He was gentle with her in comparison to how the sailors had treated her and how the white men were handling those being pushed in another direction. It was close to twilight, darkness quickly coming on. He gestured her toward the dirt track leading into the forest. He spoke to her in a dialect near to her own Kroi language, conveying enough for her to know she was to go with him. She was heartened a bit to hear some snatches of a language she was familiar with. That—and the darkness of the man—gave her some encouragement that the world she was entering wasn't totally alien to her.

Why was she being separated from the others and being led into the forest by this imposing black man? She knew why. Had she been brought all this way from her African village just to be covered in the forest here, killed, and left to rot away?

She almost welcomed that. She was covering her wrist with her hand as she walked. Through some form of miracle she still had the ivory bracelet that Otta had made for her and given to her before they had lain together that last time, only to be discovered by Otta's brother, Mingo, who went wild, beat them both, covered Isata, and then sold her to the English. Now Otta was a world away from her and she had been covered by many men. She almost welcomed death, and would have, if she didn't have such a strong will to live.

The man led her down the track through the woods for a short distance. She could hear the surf of a sea off to her right. She found it comforting to be able to hear the sea. They didn't go far before he turned in that direction and they were on a narrow pathway through the foliage. She saw the wooden fences as they reached them, which turned out to be a few fenced enclosures of maybe fifteen paces from side to side and front to back. He led her through a gate into one of the enclosures, which was floored with beaten earth. At one end a rough timbered roof extended over the floor a bit, to provide some shelter from the elements. A padded mat, stuffed with what she'd learn was boiled Spanish moss, stretched out on the floor next to two buckets, one with water, the other for necessity. A few apples and biscuits lay on a wood trencher.

He left her here, closing and locking the gate behind him. Once she was reasonably sure he was gone, at least for now—she was sure he would be back—she moved around and explored the small enclosure. Why was this here? To hold enslaved people, she assumed. That's what she was—enslaved and at the mercy of this man and more like him. Some of them were white. She had seen the look of lust in his eyes, but she wouldn't think of that now. She fell upon the fruit and used the dipper provided to drink from the bucket of water.

She no sooner had slaked her thirst and hunger and relieved herself in the other bucket than the man was back. He pointed to himself and said, "Cuffee," which she took to be his name, and she realized that he was trying to make some connection with her before he did what he wanted to do. He gestured to her, but she could not bring herself to give him a name. She wouldn't resist him, but she would not pretend that this was what she wanted. He reached out to the knot in the cotton skirt she had tied around her waist, the only item of clothing she was wearing. She looked levelly into his eyes as the skirt fell away and she could see the desire and lust in his face and hear the release of air from inside him.

She backed up and lay on the mat. He unshackled her wrists and ankles, for the first time seeing the ivory bracelet she was wearing. He stroked this momentarily but this wasn't where his interest was really focused at the moment. He let his hands move farther, stroking her arms and her belly, her legs, and between her thighs. She didn't fight him, but neither did she respond to his touch. He gently coaxed her down on her back on the mat, parted her legs, and laid between them, heavy on top of her but not too heavy.

He was still covering her when they both heard a gunshot not too far in the distance. He rolled off her and was up on his feet as fast as a jack rabbit. Just outside the gate, he grabbed up his breeches, pulling them on his legs as he hopped about, and then he reached for a rifle he'd left there, and he was gone.

He had left Isata unshackled and the gate open. As soon as she couldn't hear him moving in the brush anymore, she jumped up, grabbed up her skirt, and was out of the gate. She headed in the other direction from the one she had heard Cuffee take. She had no idea where she was going other than away. She struggled through the foliage for some time, most likely going mostly in circles, panting and gasping, before her adrenaline wound down, her strength gave out, and she sank to the forest floor. When she had calmed down, she wrapped her skirt around her and knotted it. Then she looked around in all directions, trying to decide what to do now, where to go, how to remain free for as long as possible.

When her heart had stopped pounding in her ears, she found that she still could hear the surf. The need to get to the sea became an imperative for her, and she began stumbling in that direction through the undergrowth. She saw the weak, wavering light before she came into the clearing, where a hut built of what she later would learn was tabby, the type of cement made of lime from burned oyster shells mixed with sand, water, ash and crushed oyster shells that predominated on the island, perched just inside the foliage line of a short beach leading down to the sea. The light was from a lantern inside the hut as seen through an open door in an otherwise blank wall. She must have been heard thrashing around in the forest, because, as she approached, the frame of a large, well-padded Chocolate-brown woman filled the doorway to the building.

"Help me," Isata croaked in Krio.

To Isata's relief, the woman appeared to understand her and answered in a variation of the same dialect. "What is the matter, child? Come inside. You look half dead."

Less than a half hour later, Cuffee appeared at the woman's door.

"What was that gunshot I heard?" the old woman asked him in familiar enough words for Isata to get the gist of what was being said. The woman was standing squarely in the doorframe, which she filled.

"We brought fresh slaves in today, Hannay," he answered. "One of the new field slaves broke away. He was shot. Another one, a young female, has escaped too, though. Have you seen any sign of a young female around here?"

Hannay stood solidly in the doorway, looking her son in the eye, taking her time answering him. When she had, he commanded the woman to stand aside, which she did. Cuffee walked past her and to the back of the one room that composed the cabin, to where Isata was cowering. He lifted Isata up to her feet and once more worked the knot holding her skirt together. As the skirt puddled to the beaten-earth floor, he picked the young woman up; laid her on her back on Hannay's Spanish moss-padded bed; undid and dropped his breeches; lay on top of her, and covered her again, completing what he had started in the holding pen.

Hannay stood by and watched her son breed the newly arrived slave. Knowing now that there was no rescue from the man's mother, Isata turned her face to the tabby wall and picked out the shells in the lime-based plaster with her eyes until the man was finished with her.

But Cuffee wasn't finished with Isata. When he rose off the bed, he pulled the ivory bracelet off Isata's wrist, smiled at his mother, and gave her the bracelet. He then picked Isata up in his arms and walked out of his mother's cabin. He didn't take the young woman back to the stockade, though. He walked along the beach line to another cabin, almost identical to his mothers. This cabin also had a primitive bed in it, wider than then one in Hannay's cabin. It also had leg irons attached to the wall by a chain, which he attached to Isata's ankle. In the coming days, she would find that she could reach any place in the cabin, but the chain would not allow her to leave the hut.

Cuffee then lay Isata on her back on the bed and moved his hands over her body until she groaned with a need of her own in spite of herself. In the ensuing days, enough that Isata lost count of them, he covered her again and again, every day. He was a young, fit, virile man and Isata was a beauty. Within days, she became resigned to her fate. She could not deny that he was a desirable man, if it was a man that she would have to lay with. She started receiving him as a wife would her husband.

That does not mean that she forgot Otta or what they had had together that Cuffee did not give her. She also did not forget the ivory bracelet she had managed to keep in her journey across the Middle Passage only to lose here, in the New World. The memory of it would have to continue as her connection with Otta and the world Isata had lost.

* * * *

Isata now accepted Cuffee as a wife would. But Isata was not Cuffee's wife. He already had a wife, Mercy, who had been sent over to the mainland for several weeks by the master of Oak Ridge Plantation because she was an expert in the processing of indigo and was hired out to ply her trade there. She was returning to Daufuskie Island and would expect to occupy her own bed with Cuffee. Realizing this, Cuffee turned Isata over to the white plantation overseers, begging them to sell her away because he did not think he could resist her when Mercy returned to him, and that inevitably would cause bad blood among the plantation slaves.

Thus, Isata, now with Cuffee's child growing in her womb but not showing, and after the white overseers had their sport with her, was sold to Matthew Baldwin, the owner of the Wexford Plantation on the adjacent Hilton Head Island. Baldwin was not in the need of a field worker. He was interested in acquiring a house worker and bed warmer. The beauty of Isata was such that she met his requirements perfectly. She was not yet showing her condition in ways a man like Matthew Baldwin could see, though.

The beauty of Isata was so striking that she caught the eye of Baldwin's wife, Amanda, as well, who had exotic tastes of her own. Matthew Baldwin was a refined and experienced man for his time and had always had a slave woman in his bed. From the very first night in his bed he was training Isata in the art of pleasing a man, and Isata gave in to the training, knowing that she had no other choice—that her survival depended on doing what was expected of her in this new world.

When Isata left Matthew Baldwin's bed that first night, Amanda Baldwin was standing in the corridor and beckoned Isata into her room.

"How far along are you?" Amanda asked as they were stretched out alongside each other in the afterglow.

"What do you mean?" Isata asked fearfully. She knew she was with child but she was afraid of what would happen to her if she admitted it.

"Women know these things," Amanda said. "I ask because I would prefer that it not be thought to be my husband's."

"So, you will send me away?" Isata was too frightened to think of the other avenue open to an all-powerful white master.

Amanda laughed. "I would send my husband away before you now that I have you afresh. No, we must find another way."

106

Amanda Baldwin was a brilliant woman. She found another way within the week. The ebony suboverseer of a nearby plantation on Hilton Head, Port Royal, presently owned by the Tisdale family, Jack Tisdale, was in favor with this family. Not only was he given the family name but the Tisdales were looking for ways to reward the man, who, although only in his early fifties, was getting too old to do his demanding job on their plantation.

Amanda gave him Isata as his wife, his own wife having already died. She did not give Isata to him to have with him at Port Royal. He lived at Port Royal Plantation and Isata continued to live at Wexford Plantation. One night every two weeks he came to Wexford Plantation and bedded her, and one night every two weeks she went to Port Royal Plantation to be bedded by him. At other times, Matthew bedded her whenever he wanted to and Amanda bedded her whenever she could do so without anyone but the plantation slaves knowing she did it. Nothing, of course, was a secret to plantation slaves—or to close relatives, it later transpired.

Being refined and experienced, both Matthew Baldwin and his wife, Amanda, found ways of enjoying Isata right up to when she gave birth and Isata was getting a full education on how to please men and women alike. If there was a kernel of a question in Matthew's mind whether the child Isata was bearing was his, his wife assuaged that by assuring him it was Jack Tisdale's. Completely ignorant of such things, Baldwin readily accepted that Amanda would know.

When Isata gave birth to a girl, in reality Cuffee's baby, but legally and in the eyes of the community Jack Tisdale's baby, she named the little one Otta Tisdale.

In less than a year Matthew Baldwin was dead, thrown by his horse into a marsh, where, unconscious, he drowned. Amanda Baldwin continued on as the mistress of Wexford Plantation for a decade and a half longer, managing the estate and family businesses better than her husband ever had.

She also openly—at least to those living and working on Wexford Plantation—moved Isata into her bed and the child, Otta, to a nearby bedroom. She was blatant enough about it that her extended family knew what was what, but she held the reins of power on the plantation, and thus they could say nothing and had no desire for the situation to be known beyond them.

Isata was a slave to the plantation, but Amanda was a slave to Isata and her daughter, Otta. Although they were confined to the big house on the plantation, Isata became a power in her own right, and her daughter was raised and trained as if they both were daughters to Amanda, who had no children of her own. They were taught English—both to speak it and write it properly—how to dress and how to walk. Isata was taught to help Amanda in the management and accounting of the plantation. They were taught to play the pianoforte and they were taught to do needlework and to draw. Isata proved to be a talented artist. One of the first drawings she made was of the ivory bracelet that the Otta of her homeland had given her and Cuffee had taken from her and given to his mother on Daufuskie Island. She treasured this drawing above all else, and on more than one occasion took it out, showed it to Otta, and told her daughter stories of her homeland and of her namesake.

Soon after Matthew Baldwin died, so did Jack Tisdale, and Isata no longer had an arranged husband. By now, however, she had acquired a taste for men as well as women, and when she was twenty-eight, her daughter by then being ten, Isata took a shine to a young and handsome black buck, Vandi, who worked the rice fields, who was twenty, and who was one year from having been brought across the Middle Passage from Sierra Leone. Their relationship began as sharing stories of life in Sierra Leone, with much there having changed since Isata was in Africa, and speaking nearly the same dialect. It moved into the sexual. Isata was still an extraordinary beauty and the difference in age only meant that she knew how to drive the young Vandi wild and that he was susceptible to her charms and experience.

Vandi had been in the South Carolina Colony for a short enough period to pine for home. In theory, Isata did as well, but her life had become so comfortable and satisfying on Wexford Plantation that her lamenting for the old world, and even for her long-lost Otta, had become shallow and perfunctory.

Thus, when Vandi told her of the Quakers who were offering slaves on Hilton Head stolen freedom and a voyage back to Sierra Leone and Vandi was keen to go and wanted her to go too, Isata vacillated. Perhaps it was her relationship with Amanda. Perhaps it was that Vandi, being young and lusty, did not mention taking Isata's daughter, Otta, with them often enough. And then, perhaps it was that Otta's world now was here, at Wexford Plantation, and favored her as no woman of her color normally was and that she didn't express any enthusiasm for seeing Sierra Leone when Isata brought the topic up. Whatever it was that held sway, when Vandi escaped from the plantation and, presumably, returned to Sierra Leone, Isata and Otta didn't go with him.

For years afterward, Isata, bringing out the drawing of the ivory bracelet and contemplating it, and at least superficially lamenting an opportunity lost, dreamed of what life could have been in Sierra Leone with Vandi—and perhaps even being able to locate the Otta of her youth. But she was a realist. Life was good on Wexford Plantation with Amanda Baldwin and was far more than she had a right to expect in life.

Everything was fine right up until Amanda Baldwin died and her relatives descended on the plantation to "make things right." Isata was in her early thirties then, still beautiful, regal, and accomplished. Her daughter, Otta Tisdale, was even more of all of that at age eighteen. It thus would be no surprise for that time and those circumstances that Amanda's heirs sold Isata to a brothel in Bluffton, on the mainland overlooking Hilton Head, a small but refined town where planters sent their families for the hot and muggy season and where they went themselves to play. Otta, being even more a desirable morsel, was sent to Mrs. Campbell's brothel in Savannah, although it wasn't long before she was bought again by a fabulously wealthy planter to continue life in Savannah as his private mistress and, eventually, the mother of his by-blows. Even later she opened a brothel of her own, Tisdales, which became the most exclusive gentlemen's club in Savannah.

Mother and daughter did manage to meet off and on for the remainder of their lives, but they had been trained for what they became and were resigned to it, trapped by their beauty. The one possession that Otta took with her when the two were separated on Rexford Plantation was the drawing of the ivory bracelet, made by Otta Tisdale's Sierra Leone namesake, with the admonition never to forget or fail to take pride in where she had come from—and never to stop telling their story.

~

If you enjoyed this book please let others know by posting a review, however short, and check out the other books in the

Charlotte Diamond Mysteries Series.

Where to Find Antecedent Background

- For background on how Charlotte Diamond and Brenda Boynton/Brandon met, go to Book One, *By the Howling*, chapters four and six.

- For background on Charlotte Diamond and Brenda Boynton/Brandon cohabiting and becoming intimate, see Book Two, *Retired with Prejudice*, chapter five.

- For background on Brenda Boynton/Brandon being investigated for murder and Charlotte Diamond's clearing of her, go to Book Three, *Coast to Coast*, chapter one.

- For background on the creation of the Curtain Call retirement home, go to Book Seven, *Curtain Call*.

- For background on Evan Worthington's wooing of Charlotte Diamond, go to Book Three, *Coast to Coast*, chapters eight and nine; Book Four, *An Inconvenient Death*, chapter one; Book Five, *What's the Point*, chapter five; Book Six, *White Orchid Found*, chapter four; Book Seven, *Curtain Call*, chapter three; and Book Nine, *Follow the Palm*, chapters five and seven through nine.

- For background on Douglas Dolan's wooing of Brenda Boynton/Brandon, go to Book Seven, *Curtain Call*, chapter three.

- For background on Charlotte Diamond's and Brenda Boynton/Brandon's marriage, go to Book Eight, *Horrid Honeymoon*.

- For background on Brenda Boynton/Brandon's relationship to Tony Trice, go to Book Three, *Coast to Coast*, chapters one and six.

- For background on Charlotte Diamond and Brenda Boynton/Brandon traveling with Chance and Marilyn Diamond, go to Book Four, *An Inconvenient Death*, chapter one; Book Eight, *Horrid Honeymoon*, chapter two; and Book Ten, *Fowler's Folly*, chapter one.

- For discussion of Tony Trice's Relationship with DeeDee Yance, go to Book Three, *Coast to Coast*, chapter three; Book Five, *What's the Point*, chapters two and six; and Book Six, *White Orchid Found*, chapters one, two, and six.

- For discussion of DeeDee Yance's mother, go to Book Three, *Coast to Coast*, chapter three, and Book Five, *What's the Point*, chapter five.

- For background on Tony Trice's relationship with and marriage to Michelle Minor, go to Book Seven, *Curtain Call*, chapters five, six, and nine.

- For background on the observation that there always are catastrophic weather events and deaths when Charlotte Diamond and Brenda Boynton/Brandon vacation with Chance Diamond, go to Book Four, *An Inconvenient Death*, chapter one, and Book Ten, *Fowler's Folly*, chapter one.

- For the first appearance of Talbot County Deputy Sheriff David Burch in the series, go to Book One, *By the Howling*, chapter two.

- For the first appearance of Charlotte Diamond's former FBI assistant Margaret Fancel in the series, go to Book One, *By the Howling*, chapter nine.

- Background on Brenda Boynton/Brandon's movie star-producer relationship with Aaron Woolridge begins in Book Three, *Coast to Coast*, chapter three.

About the Author

Olivia Stowe is a published author under different names and in other dimensions of fiction and nonfiction and lives quietly in a university town with an indulgent spouse.

You can find Olivia at Cyberworld Publishing.

Our authors like to receive feedback and appreciate reviews being posted at all online retailers and other review sites.

Olivia's Books

All Olivia's books, except the "Bundles," are available in both paperback and e-book.

Mystery Romance
Restoring the Castle
Final Flight

The Charlotte Diamond mystery series
By The Howling (Book 1)
Retired with Prejudice (Book 2)
Coast to Coast (Book 3)
An Inconvenient Death (Book 4)
What's The Point? (Book 5)
White Orchid Found (Book 6)
Curtain Call (Book 7)
Horrid Honeymoon (Book 8)

Follow the Palm (Book 9)
Fowler's Folly (Book 10)
Slave to the Past (Book 11)
Making Room at Christmas (Seasonal Special)
Cassandra's last Spotlight (Seasonal Special)
Blessedly Cursed Christmas (Seasonal Special)
Charlotte Diamond Mysteries 1 (Charlotte Diamond Mysteries
Books 1&2)
Charlotte Diamond Mysteries 2 (Charlotte Diamond Mysteries
Books 3&4)
Charlotte Diamond Mysteries 3 (Charlotte Diamond Mysteries
Books 5&6)

The Savannah Series
Chatham Square
Savannah Time

Olivia's Inspirational Christmas collections
Christmas Seconds (2011)
Spirit of Christmas (2010)

~